A sorcerer's treachery.
Leaves a city under seige
As cataclysmic war erupts across fields of pure magic

GOD MAGE

10TH ANNIVERSARY EDITION

SAGA OF THE GOD-TOUCHED MAGE
BOOK FOUR

RON COLLINS

SKYFOX
PUBLISHING
Fantasy

SAGA OF THE GOD-TOUCHED MAGE

GOD MAGE

4

AWARD-WINNING BESTSELLING AUTHOR

RON COLLINS

The Saga of the God-Touched Mage
10th Anniversary Edition
includes

Apprentice Mage
Rogue Mage
Champion Mage
God Mage

Skyfox Publishing
353 E. Bonneville Ave
Las Vegas, NV. 89101

ISBN-13: 978-1-941676-91-2 (Digital)
ISBN-10: 1-946176-91-5 (Digital)
ISBN-13: 978–1941676-92-9 (Trade Paperback)
ISBN-10: 1-9467176-92-3 (Trade Paperback)
ISBN-13: 978-1-941676-93-6 (Hardcover)
ISBN-10: 1-9467176-93-1 (Hardcover)
ISBN-13: 978-1-941676-97-4 (Special Edition)
ISBN-10: 1-9467176-97-4 (Special Edition)

FOREWORD: HEROES

Sticking with the theme of using great Rock and Roll things from the past in the forewords to this 10th Anniversary reissue of *Saga of the God-touched Mage*, I'll say this: if there' is a better song in All of Existence than David Bowie's "Heroes," I haven't heard it.

The whole thing is epic. The beat is eternal. The lyrics are existentially bone-bending. The vocals, as are so many of Bowie's, are ethereal. And when Robert Fripp's guitar enters, it's like the song literally goes to a different plane of existence. Not to go all overblown, but when I sit and listen to the song—I mean really focus, really listen to it—I think I'm hearing the entire point of why humanity exists.

I'm not going to say that this little saga of Garrick and Will, and Darien and all of the other friends and enemies they encounter along the way comes even close to that level of impact on the world, but I think it's fair to say that when we, as writers and every other form of artists, come to the page (or easel, or camera, or microphone, or... whatever), that somewhere deep in our minds, "Heroes" is what we are trying to create.

Or maybe just to participate in.

I am convinced that David Bowie himself was a walker of all the planes in the universe, and for that I am eternally grateful.

I am older now than when I first published Garrick's story, and quite a bit older again than when I very first envisioned its beginning. And it's fair to say that through the years a person's relationship with art changes—both consuming and creating it. I have always been someone who could stop and look for different perspectives on life. I wrote years of blog posts doing just that. Still, for better or worse, years bring perspective.

When I first wrote the *Saga*, I remember reveling in the characters and their situations. I liked Garrick, Darien, and Sunathri. I enjoyed putting them up against the powers of the world, both internal and external. I liked the process of exploring the darker sides of Garrick to the point of occasionally thinking of him as a more classic anti-hero. The whole process was mostly fun—or at least as much fun as writing can be.

I say that because, for me, writing can be quite hard, and when something is difficult, it is often somewhat frustrating. I don't know about you, but things that are frustrating are not always particularly fun.

That said, frustrating things can be resolved, and, again, for me, resolving frustrating things will eventually bring a sense of joy. That's the troubleshooting part of me shining out. I like a good puzzle you see. At the end of the day, I enjoy untangling a tough knot, and frustrating or not, completing a gnarly project always brings me an internal sense of joy.

Writing Garrick's story was a joy back then.

Reading through it again has also brought joy, but it's been a different kind of joy. It's something deeper than creation, though.

It's a feeling of belonging, I think.

In the case of storytelling, growing older has meant that finding the right path forward for a story brings me a sense that I'm understanding something deep within myself—and in doing that, finding an understanding of the world around me.

Every story teaches me something about how I look at the world.

In Garrick's case, I've seen things in the story that were already there, but of which my view has gotten bolder. Unless you use a limited definition, the idea that Garrick is an anti-hero is just wrong. His form of pragmatism does not carry ruthlessness to it. His frame of reference is not one that falls back on violent means to achieve his aims, at least not of his own volition. Garrick is, instead, a puppet made to dance by his masters. His heart is in the right place, and it remains there—at least until this point, right?

No spoilers, Ron.

As I read through it this time, I felt the plight of the everyman shining through it from the very beginning. Garrick has been, it turns out, a resistance fighter his whole life. I can see that now, even in the earliest drafts. Even in chapter one of book one, while Garrick thinks all he wants is to settle down with a girl and make his magic all by himself, he's world-weary enough to know that's never going to happen, even as he begins to dream it might.

Looking back at my life during the period of writing Garrick's story, I was feeling a lot of that in my life. At the time, I had worked in corporate America for a considerable number of years, and even though I enjoyed the fact that the company I worked for tried hard not to be high on the *evil corporation* scale, there were things it could not help being. Corporations are corporations. When push comes to shove, they are not on your side. At best, they can help you achieve a certain kind of life goal and allow you to work on and achieve things much bigger than yourself. At worst, they will drain your soul, then leave you by the wayside.

We can beat them, though, right?

We can be heroes.

I didn't write Garrick's story with any of this in mind, but here we are, leading into the final stages of Garrick's journey and as I look on it today I see how much of what was going on in my existence in the real world was pushed into its pages.

I love that.

Really, I do.

Art, no matter what you do otherwise, will exceed its boundaries. And at the end of the day, everything is art. If you Let It Be, anyway.

Which, of course, is another song entirely.

Ron Collins
Las Vegas
2025

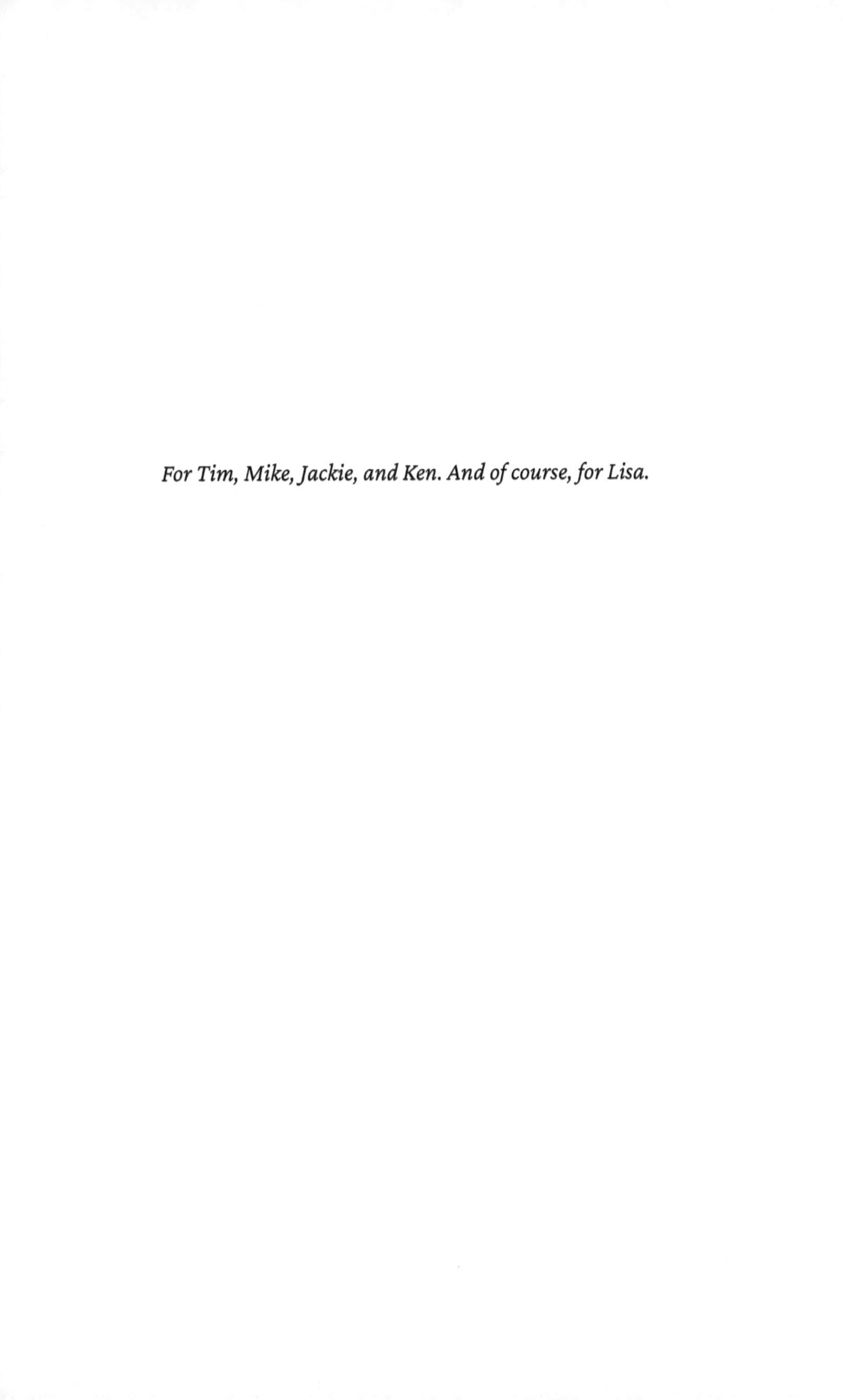

For Tim, Mike, Jackie, and Ken. And of course, for Lisa.

MAP OF ADRUIN

PROLOGUE

There are those who attack scholars who write of the Thousand Worlds. At best, they call those scholars storytellers. At worst, liars and cheats. The critics say stories of Existence, and the webs of magic rumored to be therein, are good only for children. They say those stories are nothing more than parables.

Of course, such suggestions serve merely to make the tomes these historians create that much more lucrative.

And, regardless of what one thinks of the moral strengths or failings of these scholars, it is clear that these stories resonate among the people of Adruin.

And the truth always matters in the end.

So perhaps it is important to listen to these scholars. Perhaps it is important, for example, to consider whether the Thousand Worlds actually do lie in the haphazard sprawl across the many-space that the storytellers describe, connected to one another by that flow of energy that is both everywhere and nowhere at all—the "glue" of All of Existence, as they call it. And if, as the scholars argue, it *is* All of Existence that forms the universe as it is known, as they argue, then it is All of Existence that exchanges energy between each of the Thousand Worlds, and in doing so creates the very root of life itself. For without All of Existence, those scholars say, there would be no flow, and without flow, there would be no magic, and without magic, there would be no Thousand Worlds upon which to live.

If the storytellers are right, it is All of Existence that is responsible for the sulfur worms that inhabit Gallata, and it is All of Existence that allows for the ice floes of Kanna to be a breathing species. It is All of Existence that allows for the crystalline architecture of Fallaj, and it is All of Existence that gives life to the photon painters in the realm of Gaslight.

Amid the flow, they report, live creatures known by many names.

Talla. Flow Masters. Yahli-at-ba, to some.

Gods, to others.

And, yes, planewalkers.

Yet, for all these names the scholars give, nothing is really known about these creatures, or even about All of Existence itself. This is because no other being, no man or woman from the planes—no sage or storyteller, no liar or cheat—has ever seen the world of the flow. Those who attack such scholars can do so without retribution because no other creature has ever seen Existence and returned to tell of it. No man or woman has ever been to the homelands of the creatures who these scholars argue have controlled the lives of every living creature across the Thousand Worlds since the time of Starshower itself.

No one, that is, until Garrick.

ONE

Darien shoved an undershirt into his travel roll. His sword lay across the foot of his bed, reflecting a silver gleam in the murky light of the day. The city mocked him, sprawling wide and free outside his window as if it were there for his taking. But he knew better.

The people of Dorfort saw his failure.

They pointed and whispered, and they laughed outright to his face. There could be nothing worse than being made a public fool, and he was now known far and wide as the man who had lost his order, the man who had lost his city.

Acid burned in his stomach.

He pushed a dagger into the sheath at his belt and drew a heavy hood over his head. Then he shouldered his pack.

The sword was last.

If he were any man at all, he would leave the blade here. It was a proud weapon, having been worn by his father, and his father's father before that. Its blade was etched with runes describing his family. Its steel was forged in a magical fire that bore its protections. It deserved a better wielder, but his father was dead now, and Darien couldn't bring himself to leave it. He slung the weapon over his shoulder and trudged down the silent hallway.

Somewhere, in the distant recesses of the halls, the Torean Free-born celebrated their new Lord Superior.

The weight of the sword against his back gave further proof that he was no leader.

Proof again, that he was no man.

CHAPTER

TWO

Garrick gazed out the window of Lord Ellesadil's briefing chamber. It was early morning in Dorfort, and frost still covered the rooftops across the whole of the city. It was going to be a cold, gray day. There was so much he had to do.

He was here to apologize, here to begin a new relationship between the Freeborn mages and the city of Dorfort, but he couldn't stop thinking about Darien, his friend, and the man he had thrown to the wolves the night before by taking his order out from under him.

"His" order.

That still felt strange.

Garrick had never truly led anyone before, and despite the powers he so obviously bore, he had trouble understanding how anyone, Freeborn or not, would want to be led by him. Certainly Darien wouldn't. Not anymore. Not that Garrick could blame him.

The chamber's sense of isolation and his memory of Darien combined to make Garrick intimately aware of the state of his life force—the magic, or curse, that Braxidane had planted within him. It was full and brimming over after his time in All of Existence, restless now, ready to take action. It had taken to responding in ways that were now unnerving and altogether too instinctive for his tastes. For instance, as he stood at the window now the energy inside him spread over the city on its own.

He felt fires burning on street corners below—fires in pits where people huddled to warm themselves. He sensed a horse moving over a rutted path. The odor of mud and manure, frosted with the morning snow came underneath the cover of wood smoke. He felt the vibration of the floor beneath his feet as it shook with the fall of the smithy's hammer in the manor yard outside.

These were sensations so small as to have been unimaginable before being steeped in the power of All Existence, but now he felt them all as if he were there.

He sighed.

The sound of boot steps against the wooden floor came from behind him.

Garrick turned as Ellesadil entered the chamber.

Dorfort's lord wore a simple black vest over a white tunic devoid of the usual trappings of his position. His lips were a thin line under the cover of his sparse beard.

"Garrick," Ellesadil said in simple acknowledgment as he moved to stand behind his desk.

"I apologize for my previous rashness," Garrick replied, already concerned his voice might be too sharp. "I did not mean to accost you."

"It's too late for that," Ellesadil replied, unconsciously lifting the fingertips of his left hand to his throat, that same throat that Garrick had nearly throttled the day prior.

"I hope you will let—"

"Let's be clear about something, Garrick. I don't care if you *are* god-touched. And I don't care if you *are* the high superior of the Free-born. Neither you, nor your order, can remain in Dorfort. And, if you persist in standing in my office beyond your time, I'll call my guards to have you forcibly turned out."

"Don't let one thoughtless moment on my part ruin the most important alliance on the plane."

"One thoughtless moment?" Dorfort's leader said. "You think you've made only one brash error in judgment throughout this entire play?"

Garrick winced. Ellesadil was right.

It was only a matter of time before his life force would drain far enough to be overtaken by the gnawing hunger that lived inside him. It was a dark magic, this thing within him, a dark magic that had destroyed thousands of people. His connection to Braxidane had exposed the plane to things few could imagine, and his actions had put those he loved in constant peril.

Garrick now knew that, as long as he could find his way back to Existence, he could replenish himself. And if he could replenish himself, he could keep from being a danger to those he loved. He could not, however, always guarantee he could find Existence.

Still, he wanted this to work.

"I can control it, now," he said, fighting to keep desperation from his tone. "I'm better at it."

"So wrapping your hands around my throat yesterday morning was something you did on purpose?"

"I've said I'm sorry for that."

"And you think I should forgive it because...?"

"Because I understand now that I need to serve my purpose," Garrick said. "You need to forgive me because I've finally come to lead the Freeborn as I should have earlier. And you need to forgive me because my Freeborn mages will be a force that supports the people of this city. You need to forgive me because it's in the best interest of Dorfort that the whole of my order remain here."

"Are you daft, Garrick? Seriously? Are you daft? How can you honestly think that I, being of anything resembling a sound mind, could possibly see that hosting an order of mages led by an unstable, god-touched mage would be in any way serving the best interests of my city?"

Garrick said nothing.

"Mages scare the wool from people as it is, Garrick. They don't want you here. They never have. The only reason I haven't thrown the Freeborn out of Dorfort to date is because Darien gave his word that he would control the lot of you. But now he's off his horse, and I see no reason to continue this relationship." Ellesadil paused. "Besides, I've learned something you obviously have not."

Garrick waited.

Ellesadil's face split into a broad, wild-eyed smile and he ran his hand over his hair as he looked for words.

"If you think the Freeborn can be led, you are truly insane. Your Torean mages are far more interested in their own personal freedoms than in the greater good." Ellesadil held up his hand to forestall Garrick's complaint. "Or, to give them the benefit of the doubt, they merely wish themselves to be completely free to make assess of themselves however they will. We can debate for weeks and weeks as to whether that idea works or doesn't, but the fact will always remain that the average Freeborn mage does not care about this city, and does not want to be managed."

"That's not true."

The corners of Ellesadil's lips curled upward and he gave a gentle shake of his head.

"Good luck to you, Garrick. I think this conversation is finished."

"You have to reconsider."

"No," Ellesadil said, stepping around the table. "I do *not* need to reconsider. But if I did reconsider, I might well decide to bring charges against you. I thought about doing this earlier, but prosecuting you would serve only to create a new martyr and I don't want to be the cause of whatever would come of that."

Garrick nodded. He had lost.

"How much time do we have?"

Ellesadil's gaze was steady.

"It's going to be a long winter. I want to see plans for the order's departure before the month is over. I expect you to march within a week of first thaw."

"It's fair," Garrick finally said.

"I'm glad you see it my way."

Garrick turned to leave, but paused at the doorway. "If you need anything you know where to find me."

"Goodbye, Garrick."

GARRICK KNEW he should be upset. Ellesadil had spurned his order and denigrated his mages. He should be bitter.

But this life force that boiled inside him would not allow anger to pollute his mood—perhaps he should be angry that he couldn't get mad. But instead of biting or punching, or otherwise stewing, Garrick merely walked through the government center's hallway, down the spiral stairs that swept into the grand entryway, and out of the doors that led him into the city's streets.

This was his new life. Leading the Freeborn. There was so much to do. So many decisions to think about.

He needed to speak with Reynard, of course. The thin mage was prickly sometimes, but he was second in command and he had been with the Freeborn since the moment Sunathri had birthed it. Perhaps the Torean mages could go to Whitestone, or maybe somewhere more isolated—Red Marsh to the east, or maybe south where he had grown up amid the sugar cane, maybe even the underground ruins of Arderveer.

That is, of course, if he could bear to live in a place that gave him daily reminders of his first battleground. He didn't know if he could do that, but all ideas had to be up for consideration at this point.

He stopped on the street, inhaled cold air, and watched as Dorfort came fully awake. It was a good city. It could have been a good place to grow into if he had realized it earlier. No one had ever accused Garrick of having much in the way of foresight, though. Until now, a place had never seemed to be more than a moment in time.

Yes, there was much to do.

But, Garrick knew he had to see Darien first.

The conversation with his friend would be uncomfortable, of course, which was probably why he had already delayed this long. But Darien understood Dorfort. He understood tactics and would have good ideas on where the order should go next. More than that, Garrick knew he needed to see Darien because he needed to apologize. He had stripped Darien of his order and had done so in such a visible way that Darien had to be hurting.

It had not been his intention to take command in front of the whole of the Freeborn membership.

He realized now exactly how big of a task he had, how hard it would be from this point forward. Every action he took would change the lives of those around him in ways he could not predict. This newfound weight fell upon him like an omnipresent cloud.

He sighed, pulled his cloak over his shoulders, and moved on.

Around him, it began to snow.

THREE

Neuma, the young mage who now considered herself to be the high superior of the Koradictine order, gathered her spell work carefully. The magic was similar to those she had worked before but powerful enough that failure would be painful.

Her room was lit by only a few sputtering candles. And it was small, built into the rolling hill at the foot of Mount Tara, the volcano that—if you believed the stories—was named after the only woman Commander de'Mayer had ever truly loved. Ettril Dor-Entfar, the deposed high superior, had assigned her these quarters when she was a new adept. She would move into Ettril's palace soon enough, but for now, Neuma had delicate work to accomplish and she felt more comfortable here. She considered the room to be a part of her, like her little finger, or like her liver, or pancreas. An organ deep inside that no one else could see.

There was something simple and pure about the room that made it feel right to cast this spell here. Its earthen brickwork was mossy. Thick with the smell of the island. Its roofing, thatched with saw-toothed fronds, raked the wind and raised whispers in the evenings that helped carry her mind away as she slept. A pot boiled in the fireplace, steeping sage and wild onion. Open braziers lay at each corner of the room, simmering with other spices from across the plane.

She sat on a thick mat of woven rawhide, a flat pan made of clay before her, her palms open and upturned on her knees.

Ettril Dor-Entfar's notes had been detailed, and very explicit.

She remembered them precisely.

Neuma set gates, reached for her link to the plane of magic, and trickled magestuff into the braziers. Heat rose with the aromas of cinnamon and saffron. There was darkness hidden between those spices, though, the edge of danger and fear that Ettril's notes warned would be overwhelming if she allowed them to bleed too far into this world.

She dribbled water into the pan.

The liquid beaded and ran like minnows in a pond until a slick surface filled the bottom of the basin.

Images swirled in the water. They were shadowy, irrepressible hints of a woman with hair that floated as if she were underwater.

"Hezarin," she whispered.

The planewalker came forward like an apparition—faint, and with a touch that was ghost-cold.

"I wondered when you would call," Hezarin said.

"I waited until I was prepared to serve you," Neuma replied, so pleased to know her call was expected.

"And you feel prepared, now?"

"Yes, Lordess, Highest of Superiors. I am ready to take my place at your side."

"And why should I select you?"

"I am of ranking power."

"Power can be developed."

"I am a good thinker, too, strong enough and wise enough to call you here rather than choose a different course."

"Yes," Hezarin said. "That much you have proven."

Neuma smiled, pouring more energy into the spell. She matched her breathing to the phrasing she had heard in Hezarin's inquiries. With each response, the planewalker had drawn closer, with each question she had become more substantial. That closeness told Neuma her expectation was right, it told her that Hezarin needed her. If she played this well, the Koradictine order would be hers.

IF HEZARIN HAD WANTED ONLY to see Garrick annihilated she would simply have used Neuma as her conduit rather than take the risk of walking the plane. But this was bigger than Garrick. Her brother's champion had defeated her mage at God's Tower and had now managed to destroy Ettril Dor-Entfar in Nestafar. The whole of Adruin needed to see that her powers were still strong, and the whole of Existence had to understand she would not sit by idly while Braxidane ran roughshod over her.

Hezarin would, of course, take glee in watching Garrick crumble, but as she defeated the human she would think of her brother and his dogmatically bizarre adherence to the plank of "action and consequence"—as if action was devoid of intent, and as if consequence came without guilt.

Hezarin stifled her mirth at Neuma's call.

This neophyte actually thought Hezarin needed help to step into the plane. Her naiveté was quaint. Youth was no crime, though. Neuma had, after all, managed to be among the few left standing in the rubble of Ettril Dor-Entfar's breakdown, and the idea that Hezarin could use Neuma's ambition to enact her revenge sent desire roiling through her. And, in truth, being invited did make things easier. There could be value here, Hezarin thought as she drew a protective flow of energy about herself.

The aroma of magic grew headstrong as the planewalker stepped into the room.

Yes.

There could be value in this one.

Neuma's skin tingled as mist from the braziers crawled across the floor to caress the hem of Hezarin's scarlet robe. Hezarin was the most beautiful woman she had ever set eyes upon. She was tall and thin. Her chestnut-colored hair fell past her shoulders in loose curls, and her eyes were the green of spearmint.

"You think I needed your aid to step upon this plane?" Hezarin said.

Neuma's jaw worked, but no sound came forward.

"My Mistress," she said, finally finding words. "I merely wished to support you."

Hezarin's eyes sparkled. "Come now, Neuma. You can be more direct than that."

Neuma cleared her throat. "I ... I feel I can best serve you by building the Koradictine order back to its prominence, back to the power it once was."

"That's better."

A delighted smile came across Hezarin's lips. Her voice became a cat's purr. Hezarin moved like a phantom, gliding through the misty remnants of spellwork to stand before Neuma, coiling her arm around the mage's waist to pull Neuma's body against hers.

"No secrets between us, right?" she said.

"Quite right, Lordess." Neuma bowed her head slightly, trying to contain her reaction to the pressure of Hezarin's touch. "No secrets."

"For my part," Hezarin said, gazing down at her, "my first revelation will be, perhaps my finest."

Neuma's eyes grew wide and her throat cottony as Hezarin bent to kiss her.

"Certainly," Neuma murmured before their lips touched, "it will be the most anticipated."

FOUR

Garrick arrived at Darien's chambers only to find Will standing there, clutching a collection of papers under one arm and balancing a thick stack of notebooks in the other. The boy had grown over the months, but his eyes were still his most startling feature. They glistened at him now, wide with worry.

"Where is he?" Garrick said.

"Master Darien is gone, sir."

"What do you mean?"

"He left the city last night. Reynard told me to gather up his notes."

"Gather his notes?"

"He said he wanted to see what Darien was up to."

Garrick gave a grunt. "As if Darien ever held anything back."

He looked around the chamber and saw the ornamental robes and gilded dagger that Ellesadil had given Darien during celebrations of their victory at God's Tower. The robe was precisely folded, and sitting on the dresser. The blade, wrapped in its scabbard, lay primly over it. This brought him worries. These were ritualistic symbols, and Darien came from a family that cherished such things.

"Leave the notes here," Garrick said.

Will hesitated.

"Tell Reynard that if he wants to see Darien's notes he can make arrangements for us to do it together."

"Yes, sir, Master Garrick," Will said, putting the scrolls and manuals down.

Garrick considered correcting Will's use of "sir" and "master" once again, but in this case it seemed somehow appropriate.

"Shall I go," Will said. "I still have stable work for the morning."

"Yes," Garrick replied. "You should go."

Will scampered away, and Garrick took a moment to walk around the empty chambers.

It felt cold here, cold beyond the chill of winter. The room felt of emptiness, of the hollow shiver of abandonment he had known so well growing up in the streets.

Darien had taken his demotion hard.

Of course he had.

His friend had wanted to make a difference, wanted so badly to lead his people to the greatness that he saw in them. But Garrick saw a truth about his friend now that he had not seen earlier. Darien was a leader, but he was no politician. He could achieve things that others found too big to comprehend—could make priorities and snap decisions on a battlefield, for example, and could lead armies to victory where others might find themselves buried in quagmires.

But Darien was young and he was overly exuberant. He had no patience.

He was, Garrick thought, perhaps, like his father before him.

The idea made Garrick think. He turned to examine the room once again. Yes, Darien had taken the sword his father had given him.

Another bad sign.

He may still be able to find Darien, though—at least he thought he could. Even on a horse, Darien couldn't have gotten too far with only a few hours of travel. With the sensation of life force pulsing through him now, and with the life bond the two of them had shared since the moment Garrick had saved his friend from devastation at Arderveer, he was almost certain he could reach out and touch Darien no matter where he was.

Garrick sat in a hard-backed chair and relaxed as he opened a link to the plane of magic. Sweet magestuff pooled inside him, swirling in a movement that drew every hair on his arms to the power that grew inside the chamber. He sensed people in the streets —Daventry's anger at a new cook in the kitchen, a fisherman worried about his nets hanging in the icy weather, a blacksmith pumping bellows to bring heat to fires that cooled too quickly in the winter chill.

Garrick focused to the west, then north, but felt no pattern that reminded him of Darien.

He turned his attention eastward, though, and a smile crawled across his face. He felt Darien in that direction, his heart beating warmly inside layers of protective skins. Eastward, toward the Rock Thorn Mountains where Thale, Darien's brother, had fallen to minions of the Minotaur king several years before.

It made so much sense when he thought about it.

Garrick twisted his magic, pulling a cover over himself and creating the image of a gate opening into Existence. He stepped forward, drawing more energy around him, slipping into a flow that roared with sizzling furor. Then he focused on Darien, saw where he was, and felt the area around him.

A moment later he stepped from the twisted passages of Existence, and found himself ...

... STANDING CALF-DEEP IN SNOW, the woods around him full of brittle, ice-layered trees that had shorn their leaves a month before, their branches standing firm but curling up in the cold like fingers of empty hands. Darien's horse plodded away from Garrick, its head bent downward on a snowbound path, its breath billowing in gray clouds.

"Where are you going, my friend?"

Startled, Darien drew his sword. "Garrick," he finally said.

"I didn't mean to startle you."

Darien let the blade slide back into its sheath. "What do you want?"

"I want to know where you're going."

"East."

"That is not a destination.

Darien gave nothing but an impatient glare. An awkward silence rose amid the falling snow.

"Don't be an arse, Darien. We need you in Dorfort."

"Don't patronize me."

"I'm not patronizing you. The Freeborn need you."

"The Freeborn made it absurdly clear they do *not* need me.

"All right. *I* need you. Ellesadil is evicting us. I need someone he trusts."

Darien pursed his lips. "Here is my advice to you, Garrick. Take the Freeborn anywhere. It doesn't matter where, as long as it is as far from Dorfort as you can get. This way, when the order dissolves, it will not create problems for anyone else."

"Sunathri was able to keep things together," Garrick said.

"Sunathri was special."

"You were able to manage them well enough at God's Tower."

Darien smiled. It was not the wide grin of confidence Garrick had seen so often during their travels, nor was it the grim grin of victory he had seen at God's Tower.

"You really are incredible," Darien replied.

The two stood in silence as snow fell.

"It's not my fault that I'm like this," Garrick finally said, speaking words he thought they both needed to hear.

"What's that?"

"I didn't ask to be god-touched. It's not my fault they want me rather than you."

"That—right there—is your problem," Darien said.

"My problem?"

"People won't hate you for your powers, Garrick. At least most won't. They'll hate you for your lack of conviction. They'll hate you because you have this ... thing ... about you that you could use for so much good, but you're so tied up in your own undergarments that you can't even move your bowels without thinking about it for a week first."

"I get that you're hurt," Garrick said.

Darien shook his head.

"Look at yourself, Garrick. You're standing in the middle of a snowstorm with nothing but a pair of leather breeches and a linen tunic between you and this freezing cold, a freezing cold that, I remind you, would put a normal man to the cough—yet you look as comfortable as if you're standing before a fire in your chambers."

Garrick shrugged.

"You were right to take the Freeborn, Garrick. Is that what you needed to hear? They need a man of your powers."

"You have not lost me."

Darien drew a breath and looked to the east. "Go away, Garrick."

"You know I can bring you back whether you want me to or not."

"Is that what Sunathri would have done?"

Garrick's throat constricted.

Snow fell in larger flakes. This wasn't how it was supposed to happen. Darien was supposed to forgive Garrick and say it was fine that Garrick had taken his place. *And* Darien was supposed to return with him. But he thought about Darien's words. *Is that what Sunathri would have done?* Suni had let Garrick walk free when he chose to leave the Freeborn. She had, in fact, made her point by forcing him to walk away from the order rather than be the one to walk away herself. But she had lived with his decision.

He knew what he had to do.

"You can always come back," Garrick said.

"That sounds familiar, too."

"Patience has been proven to work at times."

Darien nodded, then turned his horse away. "Don't wait too long for me, Garrick," he said over his shoulder. "It could get very lonely."

"That's a chance I'll take," Garrick said.

Then he stood silently as Darien disappeared into a cloud of blowing snow.

FIVE

Hezarin stretched.

She was lying in Neuma's bed, looking at the map she had cast upon the wall. She felt the heat of the Koradictine's body curled in a ball beside her. The map showed the path their caravan would trace across the continent over the next few weeks, ending at Dorfort, a city built at the junction of a river and a lake.

She would have preferred to just walk into the city herself until she found Garrick. There were advantages to ripping through a town—it made a point that few could miss—but she agreed it wouldn't be hard to find the Freeborn leader, and she agreed that Neuma's plan was better overall, though of course, Neuma didn't yet know how Hezarin intended to extend the approach.

There would be a time for that later.

She would savor everything so much more with Neuma involved, though, and by traveling across the continent together they would be able to place leaders in important locations and learn of areas that were dissatisfied with Ellesadil and his lazy approach to managing commerce. Dissatisfaction, she had found, was the root of all change.

And she wanted change. Sweet, chaotic change, across all of Braxidane's plane. She wanted to break Adruin, then watch as her brother attempted to avoid the fallout.

Hezarin watched the sheets rise with Neuma's breathing.

The mage had proven to be sharp and efficient. Her magic was bold. Hezarin had not seen such ambition at any time in her memory. She wondered if anything would have been different at God's Tower if she had selected Neuma as her Koradictine champion rather than Jormar.

Hezarin looked back at the map, smiling as she slipped out of bed.

She would obliterate the entire city at the end of the world, would rain fire upon it like she had commanded Ettril to do in Nesta-far. When she was done, the Freeborn would be broken, Dorfort would be ruined, and Garrick would be dead.

Yes, Hezarin thought, the trek across the land was worth it.

NEUMA LAY CURLED in a ball with her back to Hezarin. What was she supposed to do now? Her plans had been detailed but had not included falling into Hezarin's bed. Her mind raced with heady essence, and her body burned with a leaden ache that helped her know for certain the past few days weren't just a vivid dream. This thing with Hezarin complicated things, though. It left her feeling out of control, that despite the depth of her preparation she really had no plan.

She did not enjoy being without a plan.

Was she safe? What if Hezarin had used her? Had Neuma merely exposed herself to the whims of a Lordess who would later toss her aside? The idea hurt as it scrubbed against the warmth of last night's ecstasy. This was all so new to her. Did she love the planewalker? Was that why the idea of betrayal hurt so badly?

Did Hezarin feel the same?

Was this coupling more than mere gods play to her?

And, more importantly: would it happen again?

She felt Hezarin move, but she was afraid to roll over. She wanted to know the answers to these questions but realized the truth could destroy her. So she lay still and, controlled her breathing as best she could as Hezarin slid from the bed.

"You slept well," Hezarin said.

Neuma, knowing her facade was up, rolled over to see Hezarin at her ramshackle dresser, running a comb through her hair. The sight of a planewalker taking such mundane action just added to the moment's incongruity.

"Yes," she said, smiling with languid satisfaction. "I slept very well."

"It's time to begin our travels," Hezarin said.

The tone of the planewalker's voice made Neuma's belly sink. Hezarin was already focused on the plan.

Her plan, she corrected herself with a touch of anger. It was embarrassing to know she had let a single night's fling change her focus. *Her plan*, she thought. It was *Neuma's plan* to confront Garrick and his Freeborn mages directly in his hometown of Dorfort, but to do so from a traditional march across the map—avoiding the more natural, hence well-defended, bay harbor of the Blue Lake. Neuma would lead them in, creating a disturbance and destroying as much of the Dorfort resistance as necessary, then Hezarin would deal with Garrick directly.

It was a good plan, this scheme of hers, as far as it went.

It would take longer to march across the land, but once there the chance for surprise would be invaluable.

"Yes," she said, putting her feet to the ground. "They will be long days."

"And," Hezarin said, speaking with a soft tone that came from deep in her throat, "perhaps a few long nights, too, right?"

Neuma felt a grin cross her face and an odd, thrilling warmth spread throughout other areas of her body.

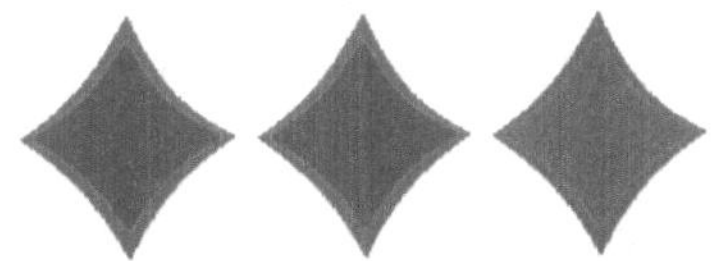

"I wish you would just let me do it my way," Reynard said.

Garrick pushed his bread away, unable to keep from glaring at the Freeborn. Reynard said these words so often they seemed etched inside Garrick's mind.

Reynard sat across from him, dabbing at his lips with the edge of a napkin. The aroma of butter and porridge lingered over their table. The hum of voices filled the Inn, which was bustling with activity because the *Dandy Mare* was outside taking on load and preparing to depart later today. The docks of Dorfort were never quiet, but they burst with energy at every arrival and departure.

This was supposed to be a simple breakfast, a way for Garrick and Reynard to get together and to be seen working in public. In hopes of creating bonds of familiarity, Garrick had directed the Freeborn to do most of their living out among the people of the city. It had worked—to some extent. At least no one had been maimed or had died in the process. But right now he would give years of his life to be able to throw something at Reynard.

He kept his voice down with great effort.

"We need a plan that holds water, Reynard. And it can't be something you just dream up and start giving directions for. We need everyone to agree. If Sunathri and Darien were here, you know that's what we would be talking about."

"You have to stop bringing her up," Reynard replied. "She's gone."

"I bring her up because her way worked."

Reynard pursed his lips. He, too, showed signs of restraining himself due to the public nature of their location. "We should just head to the Red Marshes," Reynard said. "We can live there in isolation while we get the Freeborn into better status."

"That is your pet idea, Reynard. Not a plan. What do we need to do to arrive at a plan that everyone agrees with?"

Reynard sighed. "That will never happen."

"But we can get close. Close enough, anyway. I've seen it. Sunathri and—"

"Please." Reynard held a hand up. "Sunathri and Darien, Sunathri and Darien ... I swear I hear that phrase in my sleep."

Garrick clenched his jaw. A stab of Braxidane's hunger reached a cold tendril through his thoughts. It was painful, but it was a glorious pain, a pain that made him shiver.

The hunger seemed to reach out to the sweet rush of life force he felt moving throughout the room, it snaked its way across beating hearts and rode the warm streams of blood flowing within each person here in the Inn. Garrick could taste their lives with a stifling sensation that started at the back of his throat. It made him want. It made him crave. But he could handle that now. To the greatest degree, anyway. Unclenching his muscles and swallowing down the darkness inside him, he pushed the hunger into the recesses of his being and returned his thoughts to the present.

When he recovered, Reynard was staring at him with an expression that made Garrick wonder how long he had been in that daze. He wondered if Reynard understood the exact nature of his god-touch. Was the mage just delaying everything he could until Garrick would have to leave, then be unable to stop him?

These thoughts did nothing to make him feel better.

Perhaps Ellesadil was right about the Freeborn. These mages were all the same—judgmental, vocal, and so painfully unwilling to budge from their own points of view. Unless, of course, that change came from some new perspective they had found all by themselves —which, of course, they discovered with remarkable frequency. If Garrick had wanted to spend his life soothing frail egos, he was in the right place.

Reynard was typical. Garrick understood now why Darien had struggled to work with the mage. He gave directions that were bold and directly made, but they changed on a whim, leaving the mages around him angry and bruised.

Sunathri had proven it was possible to lead the Freeborn, though, so it was up to Garrick to figure out how.

"Our plan needs three parts," Garrick finally said, raising a finger with each point. "First, a destination—a place to go where the Freeborn can agree to set up shop. Second, a set of travel plans—a map and a schedule of events as it were. And third, a preparation plan— the logistics of making it happen."

"I've already got all that."

Garrick once again swallowed the hunger that twisted through his gut.

"I will call a meeting of the order this evening to talk about locations," he said. "If nothing else we can get the list of potential destinations pared down to something I can get my mind around."

Reynard sat quietly, waves of disagreement blasting from him like the heat of a summer sun.

"I want you to call the order together," Garrick said, this time making certain Reynard could not mistake it for anything other than the order it was.

Reynard rose from the table.

"Yes, Lord Garrick. I will do that. What time would you like to meet?"

Garrick glanced outside. "Sundown."

"Will there be anything else?"

"Yes, there is."

Reynard paused as a server collected what remained of his breakfast. Garrick waited until the server left.

"I want a pair of Freeborn mages riding alongside every security patrol the Dorfort guard executes," Garrick said.

"Ellesadil asked for this?"

"No. It is what we, as the Freeborn, must do to prove our interest in the people of the city."

"I see." Reynard could scarcely contain his mirth. "Consider it done. I admit, though, that I look forward to the expressions on the faces of our brothers and sisters after they've traipsed all over the outskirts of town in this bitter cold."

"Tell them I will take my turn with them."

"They know it's different for you, Garrick. They know you will not feel the cold."

Garrick nodded. "Tell them anyway."

"All right."

Reynard walked away and Garrick gripped the table, fighting an inner battle with his hunger that no one else could comprehend. When finally the wave passed, he saw his fingers had turned the color of bone.

CHAPTER
SEVEN

As his horse stepped over a snow-covered branch, Torrance—one of the two Torean Freeborn assigned to this patrol—spat weed juice and pulled his hood tightly over his head. His ears rang with the bitter wind. He swore the juice froze in mid-air and clattered to the ground in a thick chunk.

It's as cold as a witch's ear, he thought. *Cold as a woman scorned. Cold as* ... well, so cold he thought his muscles might never unclench.

Across the way, Pedaro, a young mage from the Rock Thorns, rode on the other side of the patrol.

Ten men of Dorfort's guard tromped between them, boots breaking through the hardened surface of the calf-deep snow, weapons jangling, and voices cursing. Their coarse grumbling told Torrance they shared his disdain for both the cold and their working relationship.

He had been with the Freeborn since the early days, joining as much because he thought it might give him a chance to bed Sunathri as for any other reason, but the camaraderie of the group grew on him and he stayed even after Sunathri made it clear that nothing would ever come from that direction.

Tonight, though, he was rethinking his position.

Tonight he was cold, and he was sore.

Tonight he didn't care that Lectodinian mages were reported to have been taking action north of Dorfort. Tonight he knew this was an asinine assignment. Nothing he had seen said a Lectodinian uprising was imminent, and even if it was, who cared if they ripped a few Koradictine mages to shreds? More power to them as far as he was concerned. And, if the blue order decided to rough up a few of the Dorfort guard in the process, well, it wasn't like Ellesadil's mates were exactly an endearing crowd, anyway.

What was the Freeborn doing out here?

Garrick was a fool if he thought offering protection to these patrols was going to sway Ellesadil. They had been supporting the guard for nearly two weeks and nothing had changed. The Freeborn were still as welcome in Dorfort as the gout. The order was getting tossed on their arses no matter what they did.

He pulled his scarf down and again spat juice.

The wool of the scarf was prickly, and the whole thing came only up to his ears. It kept scratching his chapped lips. His backside hurt with each of his horse's movements. His joints ached in the damp cold. Yes, he thought, he was definitely getting too old for this.

Pedaro's breath billowed with each exhalation, too.

It was Garrick's idea that a young mage be paired with one more experienced—which, he had to admit, was a good idea. Not that it mattered tonight, though. There was no interaction to be had with the cold so bad.

A movement came from the corner of his eye.

There was something unnatural about it, yet familiar—a streak of ruddy brown, the flicker of an arm, maybe the fold of an elbow. He turned to face it just as the odor of dry blood came, and just before the spell work itself started.

Koradictine magic!

Suddenly everything became shaper, and he drew breath that stabbed his lungs.

"Weapons!" he yelled. "Pull your weapons!"

The blast crackled across the open meadow, catching Torrance full in the chest with a thunderous clap. Red fire erupted around him, and he fell backward as if he had run full bore into an overhanging limb. His right foot caught in the stirrup, though, and his horse reared in fright, toppling with the unexpected shift in weight, falling to one side with high-pitched shrieks and coming down on Torrance's legs.

His bones crunched. Pain speared his body. He couldn't breathe.

The Koradictine was on the hillside, standing in the open now, chanting with arms outstretched.

Guards ran for cover.

Torrance tried to calm himself enough to open his link to the plane of magic. Pedaro cast a green bolt toward the Koradictine, but the mage waved it away with a single, nonchalant motion, then cast a rope of fire at Pedaro. The young Torean died screaming.

The braying horse struggled and twisted on the ground, sending new bolts of pain through Torrance's leg. The leg was done for, mangled, he knew. He was too old to heal properly. Torrance ignored the pain and the bitter smells of freezing blood and horse lather as the link opened and he channeled power.

The horse managed to stand, then it bolted, and Torrance, his foot still caught in the stirrup, groaned and grunted as he was dragged along the rough trail.

He gave a cry as snow rushed under him.

His spell pooled, but he couldn't cast it.

A stone or root jarred his back. His jaw clapped shut so hard he broke a tooth. His leg stretched to the breaking point, and he screamed with pain.

The Koradictine's next spell was a cadmium-blue streak of searing fire that forked over the ground to engulf both Torrance and the horse in a single ball of flame.

EIGHT

After long travel, Neuma and Hezarin were approaching Dorfort. It was not surprising then, to come across a detail of the guard on its patrol. It was fortuitous, actually. When they destroyed it, the detail's silence would serve to hide their approach for just long enough to matter.

Now Neuma stood on the hillside and watched the Torean guard scatter. Hezarin's magic burned like razors inside her. She gathered energy at her fingertips and let loose at will, casting blue death on an old mage, then turning to the soldiers that scurried like bedazzled ants.

Never had her casting been so fluid, never had it been accompanied with such rapturous release.

She had removed the mages first, surprised that the young one had gone down so easily. And, not that it would have mattered, but she was happy the horse had dragged the more powerful of the two for so long.

Her flame work scoured on, its heat raising a thick, milky mist over the sparse woods she had used as cover. A wave of swirling blades made mincemeat of a guardsman, and she turned a thrown dagger back toward another. She cast lightning, laughing as it raised hackles along her arms, and savoring the lovely, bittersweet taste it brought to her tongue. It was citric. Orange and lemon and glory. This magic was like candy, like swimming in a lake of mage force, like walking in a cloud of power.

She cast a specter, a silver and gray woman that sang as she snaked across the snowscape to devour a man who charged up the hill. She cast a shadow, black and cold, with the touch of ice. A scream, so satisfying, came from another man, his weapon falling, disappearing into fresh snow as easily as his soul disappeared into her spellwork.

This was it, Neuma thought.

This was what she had always wanted. Life was hers. From this point forward she would take orders from no one.

And this, she thought as she stood alone amid the remains of the Dorfort guard, would not be the end.

Koradictines today.

Dorfort tomorrow.

And the Lectodinians, well, she smiled, the Lectodinians would fall in their own sweet time.

Ashgood was no coward, but if he had learned anything at God's Tower it was that no good things come from standing against a wizard with his dander up.

At the first explosion—the one that took the young, brash mage, Ashgood had taken a few running steps and dove headfirst into the snow-covered brambles behind a pine tree. He fell, tumbling farther than he expected, smashing his hand, and grazing his cheek before landing in a gully formed in the dry creek bed. He coiled there, staying still until the blast no longer echoed, then—ignoring the pain that throbbed throughout his entire body—he peered over the ridge.

A thin Koradictine mage cast killing magic, engulfing Gil and Camric in flames, and tearing into Hasi with a cloud of razors that left nothing behind but a pool of crimson-stained snow.

Even if he could gather himself to race into the clearing, Ashgood saw that any attempt to help his mates would be futile. The mage was filled with wizardlust so deep that no one who got in his way would walk out alive. So, Ashgood lay back, shivering in the gully while a trail of melted ice ran down the small of his back, and he waited while the wind carried snippets of the mage's chanting, its tone strong like an entire choir whose voices were raised and singing to the powers. Explosions and the sound of splintering wood roared out with each of the mage's spells. The screams of horrific deaths came to him, all muted against the falling snow.

Then it became quiet.

Still, Ashgood waited, suffering the trickles of snow that melted to run over his neck and down his spine to the small of his back.

A hawk whirled in the winter sky as the wind blew snow into drifts and caused branches to scritch together in rackety laughter. Ashgood's fingers grew as numb as his toes. He thought he might have cracked some ribs, and, for a moment, he considered the idea he might just die out here, alone and huddled down in this creekbed.

When he could no longer bear to wait, he eked his head over the ledge.

The only movement was that of snow falling across the clearing, and the edges of clothing, scarves, and fur, that fluttered lifelessly in the bitter wind. Ashgood crawled out of his hiding hole, watching the hillsides carefully for movement.

Seeing no signs of mages, he limped across the field.

One by one, he stopped at each of his compatriots, and one by one he found they were dead. The patrol was gone, he thought, straightening his back painfully and feeling bitter air spear his lungs.

He was alone.

He looked around and saw the falling snow had not yet grown so deep that it obscured the trail the Koradictine had taken.

It led directly toward Dorfort.

TEN

Something was wrong.

Garrick fell to one knee, his vision swimming.

All the Freeborn were here to finalize plans for the trip to Spire. They had just finished supper and were retiring to the common meeting chamber. Sound cascaded inside his head—voices echoed and ceramic plates and spoons clattered in the distance, amplified and warped by the government center's high, rounded ceiling. Garrick's stomach turned in on itself. He felt Braxidane's hunger grow hard and substantial, twisting with sibilant whispers at each turn. It was too much.

It was nearly time to step back into Existence and restore himself.

He hadn't lied when he told Ellesadil he could control this curse of Braxidane's, but control had its price and now that price was coming due. It had been too long since Garrick had given his darkness its head.

The hunger screamed in a strange, and chilling way that led him to know something was different this time, something was more than wrong. It was tinged today with a malignant hue, a tumorous, translucent sheen that glistened in ways he had never before felt.

Poison!

Yes. That was it. Poison, ugly and foreign. He looked across the chamber to see Reynard speaking with three other Freeborn, gesturing in his usual, overly animated way.

The idiot!

Garrick bought himself time by setting a gate and casting magic that turned his hunger in on the substance. Yes, it was poison. Hemlock, paired with other toxins that were designed to hide it. He felt it oozing through his veins, blurring his sight and attacking his nerves, flowing over what remained of his life force like wax sealing a letter. His toes were already numb, and his fingertips growing cold. He wrapped Braxidane's magic around the thing, and Garrick could see the poison's origin, its broad leaves curling coldly against the wind as it was harvested, dried, then ground, and slipped silently into the soup he had just consumed.

The hunger raised itself then, unbidden by Garrick, and untethered. It attacked, ripping into the poison with intent so violent he thought perhaps his blood had boiled over.

Braxidane's magic was bold and it was angry. It burned down his bones and ran through the flesh of his body like a river of fire. The effort of holding the hunger back was taking too great a toll now. Garrick's muscles grew weaker by the moment, his life force nearly spent.

He should have returned to Existence days ago, but there had been so much work to do and he convinced himself he could hold this hunger down—and he had done so, too. He had quelled Braxidane's darkness for the past several days, made it stay in line.

Until now.

Damn Reynard.

Was he really this selfish? Was he really senseless enough to poison a god-touched mage? Yes, Garrick thought. He really *was*, and he was more than that. Reynard was devious. And he was unhappy.

Reynard was unhappy the mages had chosen Spire in the first place. He was unhappy he wasn't strong enough to confront Garrick straight-on.

Garrick gritted his teeth as the mage glanced over his shoulder at him, a glance that confirmed all of Garrick's inner thoughts.

Nothing had changed between them.

The tension was, if anything, worse, and this moment of perfect clarity gave Garrick to understand that Reynard had used this gathering of the mages as an opportunity to catch him unawares. He wondered briefly who Reynard had set up to take the brunt of the accusation.

"Is everything all right, sir?" Will said, coming to his side.

Garrick felt the boy warp as he approached—here one moment, then distant the next. His young voice wavered. The sound of his boots rang out nearer and nearer, yet echoed away into the distance. Garrick's hunger stirred as the boy touched his shoulder. Will's waiflike innocence permeated his being, and the darkness twisted in his gut.

"No," Garrick heard himself mutter. *No*, he thought.

"Get away, Will! Get away!"

Will drew back but did not leave.

Garrick felt the thrill of freedom surge through the dark thing inside him as it finished feasting on the poison. It surged, and he knew his pitiful life force could not hold the hunger back any longer. It was too late. *He* was too late.

The black power rose. He felt the gate set and magestuff flow.

You have given ... Braxidane whispered with such sickening pleasure that Garrick knew his superior had been lying in wait for just this very moment.

He fell to his hands and knees.

"Run," he whispered to Will.

The boy stood rooted in place, staring at Garrick with panic on his face.

... Now you must take.

"I said, run!" he screamed.

Will ran.

Garrick struggled to his feet and set his gates. If he could hold it back for just one moment more, perhaps it would be enough that Will could make safety. Magestuff poured into his veins, and he gagged on power that tasted of raw ginger and cinnamon.

The faces of Freeborn mages suddenly turned ashen.

He cast magic, then.

His fireball erupted with a deafening roar across the hallway. The chamber filled with smoke and fire and with voices that shouted and screamed and moaned and cried out in agony. The sharp odor of charred wood came then, and his hunger yearned for the force of the Freeborn life that was now hanging in the air like slabs of butcher's beef. Members of his order, Garrick realized. He had killed members of his own order.

Without thinking, he harvested that energy. It filtered through his body with the sharp sensation of cold water drank parched.

Garrick fought against the hunger, fought against the urge to inhale them all in one maddening breath. He leaned against a table-top, feeling the life force he had consumed and pressing back as Braxidane's hunger wailed against his restraint.

He felt the movement of mages racing for exits.

Had the boy escaped? Had this darkness destroyed him? The idea was an arrow in his gut. He could not have devoured Will, could he? As these thoughts formed, Garrick saw Reynard crawling from under a broken table.

"Traitor!" he called as he stepped forward.

A look of panic crossed the Freeborn's face, and magic formed on his fingers.

Garrick pinned the assassin into a corner and felt the tide of his dark power draw toward the mage. He could strip Reynard of his life force. He had done it before.

He took a stride and reached his hand forward.

There came a distant blast, a low, rumbling explosion from somewhere outside the chamber.

Garrick paused then, and turned his head to the sound.

It came from outside the government center, from the manor yard if Garrick heard right.

Another blast rumbled. Yes, the manor yard.

Puzzled, he turned back to find Reynard had slipped away.

CHAPTER

ELEVEN

Neuma marched through town and approached the government center's gate. Dorfort was burning around her, and Hezarin's magic flared again and again.

A guard stood before her and before the gate, his battle axe gleaming in the light of fires.

"You can't come in," the guardsman said.

She channeled magic and closed her fist. The man gave a choked sputter, and Neuma cast a blast that tore a hole in the foundation of the gate itself. Snow crunched under her boots as she continued into the courtyard.

A satisfying murmur rose among the people as she strode across the manor yard. A guard raced over the expanse to report her presence. Neuma let him go. She was in no danger from the city's guardsmen, and *someone* had to tell Garrick of her arrival—though her guess was that Garrick would sense it soon enough, regardless.

A rumbling came from the government center, a blast or pounding of some sort, she couldn't tell which, but nothing else seemed to be happening, and she did not break stride.

Two guardsmen stood in her way. Neuma spoke a word and threw them against the stone wall.

An aura of magic flared from the wall above.

It was a Torean mage, probably new to the craft from the rickety way he built his link. He had run from the building and now his startled face spoke delicious volumes.

Neuma cast blue flames that ripped through the evening with a thundering explosion. The young mage gave a terrified scream that was cut short. The rumbling faded and the dust of debris died down to leave the sight of a gaping hole ripped in the upper walkway of the center's wall.

More Toreans filed into the area.

Two drew up short, and despite their surprise, prepared a spell that would knit their energy together.

Freeborn, she thought with derision. Their mages would never be as strong as those of an order, and their attempts to cast in tandem were fanciful at best.

Hezarin's magic filled her.

She built a shield, and smirked as Torean fire flowed around her. Neuma was invincible to them, she thought. Untouchable. She sang with laughter and grinned with wild-eyed fury.

She would destroy the Torean Freeborn today just as Garrick had done to her own Koradictines. She would bring the Freeborn to its knees, and then she would revel in watching as Hezarin destroyed Garrick himself.

The plane would be hers.

"Come and get what you deserve," she yelled as prismatic lightning forked from her palms to splay across the courtyard with another thundering blast. Voices rose across the pitch, the cries of children, screams of women, and the deeper groans of men. They were all the same, Neuma thought. Everyone was the same when fear overtook them. No cloaks. No veils. The aroma of scorched wood and electric ozone came from everywhere at once, and the ground rocked with the force of her magic. She had them running now. She would rule them soon and, with Hezarin beside her, she would be unstoppable.

A Torean cast fire.

Her ball of flame met it in a mid-air explosion that caused windows to rattle. She rolled black energy from her fingers and wrapped it around the offending mage, giving the spell a final tug that ripped life force directly from his body.

A door opened, and a tall man stepped out.

His black hair was grayed at the temples, and he stood with his feet apart, a blue and purple cloak heavy with golden brocade falling from his thick shoulders to cover the shape of a sword that was obviously on his belt underneath. He was old, but his body still held its angles.

"I am Lord Ellesadil of Dorfort," the man said. "And I demand you bring an end to this."

Neuma smiled.

"I grant your wish," she said.

The lord flinched, raising his arm in a useless attempt to protect himself as she cast fire that arced through the evening.

TWELVE

Garrick smelled fear, dust, confusion, and grime as he hurried through the hallway and toward a doorway that led to the wall outside. The hallway was filled with panic. City officials scurried from room to room, and the shrill voices of the servant staff filled the hallway.

His hunger screamed at him as he ran.

Another explosion shook the building.

The hunger pulled deep maws of life force from him, stealing precious energy he had gathered from the dead Freeborn. Each step was harder to take than the last, each needed more effort, more concentration, and more outright desire than the one before it. His legs nearly buckled as he ran, and he had to hold himself against the wall to catch his breath.

The blood-laden stink of Koradictine wizardry came to him before he arrived at the doorway. Voices cried out as he stepped into the bitter cold of the darkening night.

Much of the wall had been destroyed, and much of the walkway had been turned into burning tinder. But the flooring that abutted the main building was still there. From this place, high atop the government center's wall, Garrick saw bodies littering the ground. Life force hung in the air as sweet as the aroma of bread straight from the oven.

The sorceress strode across the manor yard.

She was casting.

The target was none other than Lord Ellesadil, ruler of Dorfort itself.

Garrick had no time to spare.

He gritted his teeth and pulled at his link to the plane of magic.

THE INSTANT before her blast took Ellesadil, Neuma's magic burst into a cloud of foul mist.

She yelled with angry surprise.

Ellesadil looked as startled as she felt.

She raised her gaze to the top of the wall.

"Garrick," she said with an enlightened tone.

Neuma had seen Garrick at both Caledena and God's Tower, though it had been from a distance each time. The Torean god-touched had seemed frail to her then, thin and gaunt. Up close the man looked no more threatening. He was tall and gangly with lean muscles and a mass of longish, gold-white hair. In a different situation, she might have even considered him attractive.

"I wondered when you would arrive," she said as she leaned her head back and felt energy pour into her body.

THE KORADICTINE CAST a fan of black serpents at Garrick, snakes writhing, bats wheedling, and dragons snapping with teeth of yellow flame. Garrick countered with a shield of raw magestuff.

The spells clashed with a clap of thunder so loud he cringed.

The smell of carbon and blood grew thick in the air.

"You know my name," Garrick said, placing one foot gingerly on the platform's edge. "I, however, don't have the privilege of knowing yours."

The Koradictine strutted forward, her cape flowing in the winter air. "You will know it soon enough, Garrick. As will all on this plane. My name is Neuma, and I've come to claim Dorfort for my lord, Hezarin."

"You're a little presumptuous, aren't you?" Garrick replied.

Lord Ellesadil stood defiantly in the manor yard, his jaw holding the same set it had when he was giving the Toreans their eviction notice. "This is my city, Garrick. I will handle it," the Lord called.

"Do not fear, Lord Ellesadil," Neuma said. "I'll provide you your chance when I am through with Garrick."

Ellesadil drew his sword. "I'll not be treated as a child."

Neuma cast another fiery spell toward Ellesadil.

Garrick leapt from his rail, catching his fall with magic and deflecting the Koradictine's spell as he landed between the two. Neuma's fireball impacted at the lord's feet, and the explosion threw Ellesadil through the air and to the ground where then he lay without motion.

Garrick dug into his dwindling pool of magic and turned toward Neuma, but the Koradictine was ready for him.

A golden blast threw him backward, hard against a mud brick oven. The back of his skull cracked so sharply that his vision swam. He slumped to the ground, dazed. It took everything he could muster to roll to his knees. The Koradictine was fast, though, and she was strong. He had been wrong to underestimate her.

He rose painfully to his feet.

He had nothing left, and the blackness inside him pounded against his head.

It wanted out, it *needed* out. But Garrick saw what would happen once Braxidane's magic had its head.

He imagined himself cutting a swath through the city, burning buildings, destroying people, and filling himself beyond the point of bloating with the life force of the dead.

He swallowed the idea down, feeling it stick in his throat like a wad of dry straw, but the all too familiar ball of the hunger's malignant patience fought him, its aura born of the instinctive knowledge that Garrick could not defeat it forever, and the certainty that every postponement merely served to drive it to greater heights in the end. He remembered the village of Sjesko and the hundred lives he had taken. He remembered the tunnels of Arderveer. If he let the darkness loose now he shuddered to know the damage he would render to a place the size of Dorfort. Yet to hold it cost him dearly, and he needed to deal with this Koradictine.

"I have Hezarin's aid," Neuma said as she stepped nearer. Her expression was a clot of gloating and masochism. "I cannot lose."

He glared upward with bloodshot eyes.

"Beware of planewalkers," he said. "They've been known to stretch the truth."

Neuma's hand rose, and a sizzling cone of blue fell over Garrick. Only his casting of a reflexive shield kept him from a grisly end. He pulled on his link and cast a frail bolt of energy at the Koradictine. It missed, but gave him a precious moment to breathe.

A small, female voice came from across the way.

Amanda, the young Freeborn. She chanted.

Her magic swirled, and a green lasso rose above her head. It looped around Neuma, tightening over her shoulders and holding her arms to her side.

Neuma laughed, then.

"Surely this is a joke," she said, shredding the restraint with a shrug of her shoulders, and wheeling to cast the same spell back at Amanda, who fell to the ground, writhing and wriggling, unable to break the bonds. "If you're going to cast a spell," Neuma sneered, "at least have the decency to cast it well."

Then came Seao-da, a wizard who had joined the Freeborn only in the last fortnight. He cast a bolt of energy that lit the tattooed patterns on his face, but that shattered in mid-air.

Neuma twisted her hand and Seao-da fell to his knees, wordlessly clutching his chest.

The Freeborn, Garrick thought. They were coming for him— some of them, at least, the few who truly believed in Sunathri's original vision.

He stood as best he could.

His back hurt, but he ignored the pain to pull what magestuff he could manage from the plane of magic and cast it into defensive spells that slowed Neuma's advance.

The Koradictine threw another ball of fire in his direction.

Garrick deflected it.

The sparking debris fell into a row of corded wood, hissing and smoldering in the darkness. Another bolt of lightning came, then another. Garrick turned them each away, but the work numbed his arms and his shoulders felt like they were on fire.

He fell back, his hunger growing black and cold.

As he stepped away, his glance went to the window of his room. It was an unconscious movement, one he had done ever since Ellesadil assigned him to the space. Before, though, that glance was filled with wonderment of how he had risen from his lowly position as a street urchin to fill such a place.

Today he saw something different.

Today he saw the shadowed face of Will, standing there in slack-jawed concern.

Neuma grinned as she followed his gaze.

"I see," she said, whirling to cast a looping rope of fire toward the opening.

"Will!" Garrick yelled.

The boy disappeared behind the window just as the fire struck, and Garrick had no way to tell if he was hurt or not.

He dug deep, though. He gathered the tiny scraps of what energy he still had into a nexus point. It didn't matter, he thought. This hunger that flashed with a quicksilver edge in the darkness of night was nothing less than the corruption of the planewalkers themselves. The darkness was coming no matter what he did, and it would wreck its devastation through him no matter what he wanted.

Somewhere, Braxidane was giving that wry chuckle of his.

But Garrick could at least do this one thing. He could at least rid the plane, and his Freeborn siblings, of this one Koradictine menace.

He screamed then, and he raced forward with a vision of utter clarity, throwing everything he had into this last raw burst of power.

Neuma backpedaled toward the government center's entry gates, grinning.

"That's more like what I expected, my friend," she said.

She twisted her hands, casting a whirling set of spinning balls on a connective rope.

The contraption twisted around Garrick's feet and pulled them together. He fell into the snow, his face buried in a drift, his head swimming with fatigue. It was hard to breathe. One of Neuma's boots filled Garrick's vision. The cold flash of a shark's movement turned inside him, and he felt her life force pulsing like a beacon, so near. So near.

"You are weak, Garrick. That's why the Torean order was fated to fail from its very beginning."

Garrick rolled to see her better.

The air became choked with the thickest smell of blood magic he had ever felt.

Hezarin.

She appeared a ways from Garrick, radiant and thin, her red dress flowing about her, maroon henna curling up her arms and over her forehead.

Neuma's gaze flickered to the planewalker. She smiled.

"You are just in time, my Lady," Neuma said.

A glint came from behind Neuma. A simple flash of lavender in the winter gloaming that Garrick thought was somehow familiar.

The sound of steel in flesh punctuated the moment, and Neuma gave a grunt as a sword blade suddenly protruded from her chest.

Neuma's eyes bulged, and she fell to her knees.

Behind her stood Darien, and behind Darien was the tall outline of a guard Garrick knew was named Ashgood.

"Save me, Lady," Neuma said to Hezarin, as she stood there on her knees, frozen in time but tottering, the words bubbly in her chest.

Hezarin's smile was wicked and cold.

"You served me well, Neuma. You've left Garrick right where I wanted him."

"But?" she responded.

"You've proven to be devious, though," Hezarin said, spellwork crackling on her fingertips as she brought them to Neuma's face. "You kill off more of my mages than I do." A single beam of scarlet lit the evening. A hole burned through Neuma's forehead, and she dropped facedown to the ground.

In the distance, Amanda, her bonds broken with Neuma's death, scuttled away, and out of the manor yard.

THIRTEEN

Garrick tried to get away, but he had no strength. His hand slipped in the mud, and he felt the sudden sting of the winter cold. Hezarin approached, gliding like a cat, the pupils of her eyes drawn wide.

Darien stepped between them, his sword flaring purple, its etched runes writhing along the blade. "You'll have to kill me first," he said to the planewalker.

"That can be arranged," Hezarin replied, casting magic at him.

"Darien!" Garrick said, throwing the dregs of his life force into a shield around his friend.

The impact sent a curtain of sparks dancing across the grounds.

Hezarin wailed in frustration and pointed a finger at Ashgood.

The man died before he knew what was coming.

Darien glared at Garrick and pushed against the barrier. "Let me out," he said.

"I can't let you die for me," Garrick replied. He stood alone and exposed as Hezarin turned like a black widow at the end of her web.

"Protect your friend while you can, Garrick. Funnel your power to him as you will. But I will kill him after I'm through with you."

A fist of power crashed into Garrick's chest. He fell against an open wagon and reached desperately to the wooden wheel to keep himself upright.

"Braxidane!" he yelled. "Braxidane!"

"My brother cannot help you," she said. "I've played his own game against him and brokered deals with half the powers in Existence. He cannot come to Adruin now and expect to live."

Garrick tried to breathe but drew little value.

His vision danced red.

She was playing with him, now. She could kill him any time she wanted.

"Why do you care about this place?" he was finally able to whisper.

"Once you're gone, Garrick, I won't care about it at all. Neither will anyone else in Existence. I may just raze it when I'm done."

Garrick's stomach clenched.

Magic wafted above Hezarin as she moved toward him.

He reached for his link, reached for life force, reached for anything that would give him strength. But he was done. There was truly nothing there but his hunger, and that hunger rose inside him in ways that were all too familiar. He felt it filling him, felt it giving him its ugly power.

In the distance, Ellesadil stirred like a man coming off a three-day drunk.

Fire flared from Hezarin's fingertips.

Garrick drew on his hunger to pull a shield over him. Rather than deflect the planewalker's magic, the hunger absorbed it as a sponge takes on water. The heat was intense, and when it was done a harsh smell of singed oil lingered.

The planewalker gave a smile of victory. Magical residue burned around her.

"You are nearing your rage," she said.

Hezarin's expression told him she knew everything about him, how when the hunger rage hit he would be uncontrollable. And he knew now that when that happened she would merely step aside and let him do her damage for her.

He had only one choice—retreat into Existence.

It would mean abandoning his friends to Hezarin's whim, leaving them defenseless. What would they think of him when they saw him leave?

It didn't matter.

He understood the trade-off, a few lives here for hundreds or thousands there, and he knew what he needed to do. It was the only option that would keep the city of Dorfort alive.

Garrick pulled his link, and at the same time let his darkness out to drink the life force of guards and mages alike. He felt them as he used them. Their desires were pristine, their fears powerful. He searched until he found a portal.

The gate to Existence was easier to open this time. Easier to approach.

His hunger wailed as he leveraged it. It raged. It screamed. It beat its writhing essence against Garrick's chest at the unfairness of his ploy.

But, still, Garrick stepped into the portal.

The door closed, and then there was only the flow.

Hezarin, too, wailed.

Anger scoured every part of her being. Raw, bitter anger. Anger of passion. Anger of betrayal.

Where had Garrick gone?

The truth dawned a moment later.

There was only one place he could have gone. Of course. And she wasn't going to follow him there. Not, yet, anyway.

She felt movement in the web of magic she had laid behind her.

It was Darien, sword drawn. Her spellwork was quick and clean. She wrapped her senses around him and squeezed.

His motion came to a halt, his blade remaining suspended in the air.

Then she smiled as a new thought struck her, a thought so gorgeous as to send a shiver of anticipation across her shoulders.

FOURTEEN

Will raised himself from the hallway.

The blast had thrown him clear across Garrick's chamber and destroyed much of the room. The stone here was cold, and his cheek throbbed where he had crashed to the ground. He saw the nearly full moon through the blast hole as it hung like white fire over the horizon.

He crawled to the edge of the room and peered once again out over the manor yard. Wild odors came from below, blood, and honey, and the thick, electric smell of lightning after a storm.

"Get inside Karl," a woman's voice yelled from somewhere down in the manor.

"Wallace!" another said.

A door slammed, and window shutters squealed shut. Footsteps scuffled, and the metallic jangle of the guard seemed to come from all directions at once.

Will grabbed an exposed rafter and swung out to land on the walkway around the government center's wall. Then he stared over the railing.

Garrick was nowhere to be seen.

Hezarin stood before Darien. Her voice rang with a sorcerous tone.

Darien stood artificially still, his blade poised as if in mid-slash.

Knowing only that something was terribly wrong, Will scooped wet snow together. It was too cold for a proper snowball, and his fingers went quickly numb, but it came out solid enough that he could unloose the white missile. It struck the sorceress perfectly in the small of the back just as her magic was about to be released.

She gave a startled jump.

Darien fell to the ground and began to crawl toward her.

The woman's gaze raised to Will's, black like coal. She swept her hand toward Darien, though, and he drew still once again.

Will ducked under the railing and tried to ignore the serpentine fear that was crawling up his arms and his legs. He began to shiver. He had to move or he would be a goner.

He kept his head down but scrabbled in a direction that brought him closer to Darien.

"Leave this city, now," Ellesadill's voice rang out from below.

Will grimaced.

The Lord had gathered himself and was now standing his ground. Ellesadil was a fine statesman but this work called for a swordsman or a mage, and the lord was neither of these.

"Are you serious?" Hezarin replied.

"Guards, to my side!" Ellesadil called, but there was no apparent response.

The coppery smell of blood grew bolder, and Will could easily imagine the sorceress's magic circling her head like poison.

Garrick would be back, he thought.

His master wouldn't leave them here alone.

Will believed that with all his heart. He had believed in Garrick from the first day they had met, back when his superior had promised to keep Kalomar, his horse, from harm. Garrick had spoken to him like an adult, then, and had come back to save him. Garrick had come back to Caledena, and he had come back to get him when

Will was caught by Ettril. Garrick had given him everything he had today.

If there was one thing Will was certain of in this life, it was that Garrick would come back again—and that when he came back, he would save the day.

Will just had to keep the sorceress occupied until that could happen.

He just had to give Garrick time.

The walkway here was leeward and had no snow nearby, but a row of icicles hung from the cover above him. He leaped and grabbed one, but his action shook three others loose and a crystalline shower clattered down on him. Only his immediate dive and scramble around the corner saved him from the ball of flames that erupted where he had stood.

He jumped to his feet and rained icicles like daggers down on the sorceress. They missed, but they gave him a moment to dive away from his place, and by the time Hezarin had twisted from them and spoke her spell, he had ducked behind a different railing. Still, if the stone had been only half as thick, he would surely have been killed.

Will fell to his stomach and wormed his way toward a guard post where he saw a blade and bow propped against the wall.

It was cold.

So very, very cold.

But if he could get to those weapons, perhaps he could make something else happen.

If he could get to them, perhaps he could give Garrick just a little more time.

Hezarin looked at the smoldering remains of the guard post and pursed her lips.

That should do it for the boy.

She turned her attention back to Darien, twisting her magic and feeling him struggle against his restraints.

In short, jerky motions, she stood him up.

His blade felt cold against her spell. Its magic repelled other magics, but it had never faced a casting as powerful as hers.

DARIEN FOUGHT AGAINST HER COMMANDS, but his muscles cramped and his skin felt like it had been set on fire. His stride came in jerky motions, every movement hard and painful, every step tearing muscle against bone. He panted with the struggle to control himself, bitter air scoring his lungs. He was losing, though, and as he grew exhausted, his body followed her commands more easily.

He should have known better than to come back, but Ashgood had said the city was in danger and he couldn't have lived with himself if he hadn't returned. Now, Ashgood himself was dead, the Freeborn order destroyed, and the courtyard commanded by this Koradictine sorceress.

And Garrick, of course, was gone.

HEZARIN WATCHED AS ELLESADIL APPROACHED.

His thick cape was blackened with mud, and he held his sword in both hands. "You've had your warnings," he said, his words emitting clouds of frosty breath.

With a rolling of her hand, Hezarin turned Darien toward the lord. His sword was raised, gleaming with streaks of magenta that seemed to intensify with each of his strides.

"No!" Darien groaned. "No!"

His sword flashed toward Ellesadil.

Ellesadil's eyes grew wide and he raised his blade to counter. Blue sparks flew as steel clashed on steel. "What are you doing, Darien?"

"Argghhhh!" Darien replied.

Hezarin spun him around, and he realized he was positioned perfectly to guide a sword's slash straight into the lord's exposed belly. Darien pulled up so hard he thought his muscles may well have stripped off bone. His hands twisted and the blade's edge rose enough that the flat of the sword struck the lord with a thud. Ellesadil grunted and fell to one knee.

Hezarin laughed at Darien's struggles.

He was like a fish on the line, his runs against her force providing her a thrill, the silver flashing of his scales showing as she pulled him through the darkest water.

"You can't save your lord for long, Darien," she said as she twisted his body around.

Darien had no strength left.

The sword dangled now from one hand.

The lord lay on the ground, trying to claw his way to the building. His breath obviously gone, his face red with defeat. Darien caught the lord in two strides and pushed Ellesadil over with a muddy boot so that he lay defenseless in the muck.

Damn Garrick! Darien had trusted the god-touched mage, and the coward had abandoned him again. This time Darien would pay for his faith in a way more gruesome than he could possibly imagine.

Tears of humiliation glittered in his eyes.

"I am sorry," he said to Ellesadil. "I am so sorry."

Hezarin laughed harder.

He fought her with everything he could muster. His muscles ripped. Starburst patterns of pain exploded in his head. But it was no use. The glint of Darien's sword flashed off Lord Ellesadil's face as he raised the blade above his shoulders.

WILL's bare fingers burned against the cold floor of the walkway. He reached up for the bow and grabbed a handful of arrows. The wood was heavy and stiff. His teeth chattered and his body shook with uncontrollable spasms.

He bent the bow under his arm to string it.

His fingers barely worked, but he managed somehow. He picked out an arrow and nocked the bolt against the gut. It took him three tries to get a firm grip, but when it was finally there, he stood up and took a quick aim.

The scene below nearly stole his breath.

Darien pounded the flat of his blade into Ellesadil's ribcage, and the lord fell to the ground. Hezarin laughed and spoke, but the wind carried her words away.

Darien prepared for what would surely be a killing blow.

Will trembled. The wind bit at his cheeks and stabbed dry daggers into his eyes. He pulled the bow as far as he could. His aim jittered. Clenching his jaw, he lined up his target and let fly.

The arrow buried itself in Hezarin's shoulder.

She screamed a wild banshee's scream, and even from this distance her eyes now locked onto Will's.

Her hand went to her shoulder, her magic melting the shaft and absorbing it into herself. Darien fell to his knees first, then he pitched sideways into the snow, his sword tip embedding itself before Ellesadil's feet.

She turned her magic on Will, then.

Gory beasts sprung from the walls around him and from the floor below, monsters whose skin ran with venomous ichor and whose distended jaws clacked with serrated fangs. Wind raged. Will grabbed the bow and whacked the closest creature over the top of its head. The weapon splintered, but the monster moved back, giving

Will the opening he needed to leap to the top of the city wall and tightrope away.

The beasts did not relent, though.

A green-black serpent with putrid yellow eyes and fangs that were curved and bathed in icor, raised its hooded head.

Will waved the broken stub of the bow before him like a dagger, glancing downward over his shoulder. The fall on the other side of the wall was easily five floors.

He was done for, but he preferred a fall from which he might recover to suffering what this beast would do, so Will closed his eyes and bent to leap.

His only thought as he rose into the air was *I hope I've given Garrick enough time.*

FIFTEEN

A waterfall's rush of pure energy flowed over Garrick. It crashed against his hunger, splattered against his body, and rolled off his skin like he was oiled parchment. Everything ached. Everything burned.

But through the pain, his skin yearned for the current's fire. His flesh cried out for its strength. His bones gave coarse, bittersweet grinds at their joints that were half pain and half ecstasy. Cycles of life filled him as he drew on the flow—pain, rebirth, sustenance, and death. Hair raised on his arms. Heat rose in his flesh. He opened his hands into the flow to feed on its currents, and as he fed, the hunger that raged around him abated to a simmering pool of carnivorous intent.

"You are a lucky man," Braxidane said.

"I suspected you might show up now," Garrick replied.

The planewalker floated everywhere at once, a presence massive in the flow, hanging in Existence like a net that spanned the distance as far as Garrick could feel. A green finger of lightning traveled along his being, disappearing into the distant horizon.

"I would have helped you if I could," Braxidane said.

"You lie so well you fool even yourself," Garrick replied. "But I know you better than that. You would have helped if it was in your best interest."

"You don't understand what you're talking about."

"I understand well enough."

Garrick pulled his hand from the flow and felt the smugness of Braxidane's smile without even seeing it.

"We are quite well matched," Braxidane said.

"I am not like you."

"Is that what you most fear, Garrick? That we are alike?"

"Be quiet, Braxidane. I still need to deal with your sister on Adruin. And unless you plan on helping me, you're just in my way."

"That is no way to speak to your superior."

"You should listen to yourself sometime, Braxidane. You haven't done a single thing as my superior."

The energy that was Braxidane turned a faint shade of rose.

"I've taught you by providing experience."

"Do you know what I think, Braxidane?"

"This should be good."

"I think the whole thing is a sham. I think superiors are a crutch. I think a person who wants to learn magic, who truly desires to learn it, will do so all on their own. And I think true knowledge comes only when you are free to find your own powers."

Braxidane's silence told him he was right.

The world around him seemed suddenly bigger.

The currents of Existence slowed, and he saw the juxtaposition of life force and sorcerous energy for what it truly was.

Magic was everywhere.

Magic was everything.

Portals loomed about him like targets. He could go anywhere he wanted, cast any magic, be anything. He saw the shimmering gap that led back to Adruin.

"I don't need you, Braxidane," he said. "I don't need you."

As he said this he felt a surge of power so bold it nearly crushed him. It was absolute control. It was freedom. It was, perhaps, true liberty.

Braxidane drew himself to something solid, and Garrick felt a gaze that might have been awe.

Braxidane gave a subtle shimmer. "You are going to confront Hezarin?"

"Of course."

"Do you realize what will happen if you kill her?"

Garrick flexed his fingers. The energy of Existence flowed through him, and the aches in his joints faded as he soaked it up.

"I don't care," he said.

"You will."

"Why are you always putting your problems onto someone else?"

"It will be your problem soon enough. Believe me."

Garrick ignored him.

Braxidane shimmered once more. "Just know that if Hezarin dies while on a plane, it is permanent."

Garrick smirked. "All I hear in that advice is that if I destroy her, she can't return to plague us."

Braxidane laughed.

"What?"

"Nothing, Garrick. It's nothing."

"I'm tired of playing your games, Braxidane. Either tell me what you're thinking or hold your tongue."

"As you would," the planewalker said.

Garrick paused, hackles rising on the back of his neck. Assuming they were still alive, Darien, Will, Ellesadil, and the whole of Adruin needed him. He couldn't afford to get caught up any further in this game.

He gathered his energy.

"I would love to pass time with you, Superior. But I have friends who need me—please do your best to understand."

"I'm sure we will continue this discussion later," Braxidane said.

"Perhaps," Garrick replied. "Or perhaps not."

He turned away from the planewalker and stepped into the portal that led to Adruin.

CHAPTER

SIXTEEN

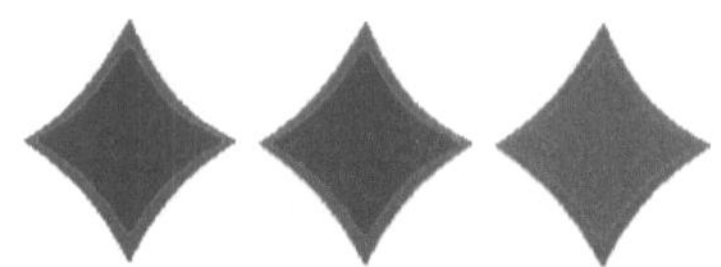

Will felt the weightless moment at the crest of his leap.

Then the ground pulled at him.

He was going to die.

He realized this as he fell, faster and faster, his arms flailing, his hands and feet grasping with panic for holds in the nothingness of the nighttime cold. He realized it as the shadow-covered ground rushed at him like an unyielding hammer.

He opened his mouth to scream.

Then a sudden force cinched around him, crushing his ribs like a huge fist. He felt heavy for a brief moment, then he was being lifted into the air. Was this Hezarin's work? Was she delaying his pain for her gratification? He struggled against her binding.

He twisted to scream at her, but his voice stuck in his throat when he saw Garrick standing atop the walkway.

Garrick, Lord of the Freeborn, glowing with starshine against the dark of night. Garrick, god-touched, depositing him safely on the ground outside the government center wall.

Garrick, Will thought.

Garrick had returned. Garrick had saved him.

Just as Will had known he would.

Will stood knee-deep in a snow bank.

The cold came back in full then, but Will ignored it. He felt the bottoms of his feet against the frozen ground below, but he didn't care. He ignored the bitter wind that seemed to be everywhere at once.

He looked up to the deepest part of the sky above, that place where he had just been falling from, and he heard Garrick's voice echo.

His heart beat a rapid-fire rhythm, and he thought for a moment that his chest might burst.

"Garrick!" he pumped his fist and called as the mage turned to join the battle. "Garrick!" he pumped again and called again as the mage disappeared on the other side of the wall. "Garrick!"

Suddenly the boy found himself crying.

SEVENTEEN

G arrick leapt from the wall and landed in the manor yard below.

Snow drifts melted around him, raising clouds of silvered mist that faded into the darkness.

Darien looked up from the ground, his eyes crimson and bloodshot.

Hezarin's face became a twisted mass as she cast a river of fire at Garrick.

He splayed his hands and ran life force through gates to meet it. Steam hissed and popped with an earsplitting boil. It was an easy magic now, effortless—his standard gates fell into place almost without thought, and the energy of Existence flowed with obeisance he had never felt before.

He planted his feet before Hezarin with a new sense of confidence.

"This is my plane," he said. "Get out."

"Never."

She growled and threw magic at him, creating wheeling discs with serrated edges that gave earsplitting screams as they arced through the air. He stood his ground, deflecting them left and right.

The planewalker's desperation showed in her gaze, then. She hesitated, then reached her magic toward Darien, who was still defenseless on the ground. He gave a deep groan of pain.

"It's you or him, Garrick. Which one of you dies?"

Garrick paused. "I've given you your chance, Hezarin. Let no one say otherwise."

The planewalker grunted. "I'll take that for your answer."

Darien gave a garbled groan.

Garrick raised his hands and a vortex of energy rose around him. The wind became a gale, and every fire in the vicinity bent toward him. Hezarin's magic shredded into fragments and spiraled into Garrick's vortex. And Garrick fed on it, drinking it as a steady stream, molding it with his hands, his fingers moving over it like a weaver's dance across the loom.

Hezarin gasped for breath. Her eyes widened as Garrick brought his spell to its end.

He dropped his hands.

The wind halted.

Darien fell free.

Snowflakes dropped in casual silence.

Then Darien shielded his face, as did Ellesadil.

But Will, who had run to the government center's front gates, watched it all.

He watched as the planewalker screamed in agony, watched as Garrick reached into Hezarin and pulled her life force into himself, watched as she buckled at the knees, then the waist. He watched as Garrick drew her in with a breath that grew deeper and deeper, an inhale that seemed to never end.

Will watched as Garrick's entire body pulsed crimson and golden and blue and black, watched as Garrick destroyed the planewalker and took on a power like none had existed since perhaps the dawn of Starshower itself.

CHAPTER
EIGHTEEN

The scars of battle smoldered in the cold darkness. Voices sounded in the distance. Fires crackled throughout the city despite the damp snow.

Garrick stood in the courtyard, the aura of power fading, but not quite dissipating. He felt the pull of the city and heard cries of the wounded.

Power coursed through his senses.

He felt fullness. Intense warmth bled from every pore.

Darien used his father's sword to help him stand up between Garrick and Ellesadil.

"I'm glad you returned," Garrick said to him.

"I came back for the city."

Garrick saw Darien's hurt then, the depth of the humiliation Garrick had caused. Yet could not miss the fact that still his friend would die defending Dorfort. "That's a good reason," Garrick replied. "Dorfort has always been more worthy of your regard than I am."

Silence roared between them.

Garrick fought the elements of Hezarin's life force as it settled inside him, and felt the wall of need he felt building over the city.

There were injured in Dorfort's streets.

There was pain.

He felt it all and rubbed his hands together absently as he steeled himself against the turmoil it caused inside his mind.

"What have you become?" Darien said.

Garrick shrugged. "I am who I always have been."

"It's untoward to pretend, Garrick."

He was right. Darien had always been able to see under his skin better than Garrick could himself.

"I am god-touched," he said, accepting that term in ways he hadn't before. "But I am still a man. No different from you in any way that matters."

Lord Ellesadil cleared his throat to draw attention. He held his damaged arm against his ribcage but still managed to place his weapon back into its sheath. He looked at Garrick.

Around them, the city burned.

"I think we should gather our wits." He looked at Darien. "I suggest you collect the guard and take action to stop the blaze."

"No," Darien said.

Ellesadil started, unfamiliar with such disobedience.

"I cannot direct your guard," Darien said.

"What?" Ellesadil cried.

"I nearly took your life, Lord. I've disgraced myself."

"I'll hear nothing of that. You *saved* my life. There is no man alive who could have done better in my service." Ellesadil paused and found just the right inflection. "You belong in Dorfort, Darien J'ravi. I've needed a commander of my guard since your father passed, and I'll accept none other than you."

Darien paused, his expression torn.

Ellesadil glanced at Garrick. "What do you think, Lord of the Freeborn?"

Garrick was suddenly jealous. Darien had a home, a place to be. His entire life had been about Dorfort, and now he would be tied to the city in the most meaningful way he could imagine.

"I think the J'ravi name will sound good in that post again."

Will ran to Garrick, then. The boy threw his arms around Garrick's shoulders, an act that showed exactly how much Will had grown over the past year. When Garrick had first taken the boy in, Will's hug would have been around the waist.

"Garrick, sir! I knew you would come back!"

He was shivering.

"You need to get inside where it's warm," he said, running his hand over Will's head.

"I'm all right," Will said.

A current of Hezarin's life force swelled toward the boy. Garrick pushed it away, looking hard at him. Will was in that awkward age where he needed true guidance, not the second-hand mentoring Garrick had been providing so far.

"I'll take Will inside," Ellesadil replied, rubbing his arms now against the cold. "We both need to get out of the elements, and I could use his help securing the center."

"Thank you," Garrick said.

"Come along," Ellesadil said to Will.

Will gave only a perfunctory argument as Ellesadil put a hand on his shoulder and led him inside, leaving Garrick alone with Darien. The two of them watched Ellesadil and the boy disappear through the doorway.

The sounds of voices grew in the nighttime.

Garrick looked at his friend. "I'm sorry," he said simply.

A neutral smirk crossed Darien's bearded face. "We're fine."

Garrick looked to the destruction around them and felt the pressure of Dorfort's panic rising. "I think you have a city to save."

"You mean, *we* have a city to save, right?"

Garrick clenched his eyes shut against the pressure and listened as Hezarin's power roiled inside him. He thought his head might explode. He could use her energy to save lives tonight. He could use it to heal. But he didn't know if he could trust it. He didn't know if he could trust himself. What would happen if he drained himself too far after he had absorbed a planewalker? Would his hunger's pendulum swing back even further than it had in the past? And if it did, could he stop at merely the destruction of Dorfort?

"The people need you," Darien said.

Garrick shook his head. "No, Darien. They need you. If I stay here now, I fear the city will suffer."

Darien took in the devastation that was the government center —the dead guardsmen and mages, the destroyed walls, and the burnt buildings. "Look around, Garrick. It will take months to make these repairs," he said. "You, and the Torean order, need to stay in Dorfort."

Garrick shook his head again, harder this time.

"If this has taught me one thing, it's that I cannot lead the Freeborn."

The sounds of the people rose over the roar of burning fire.

In the distance, the guard was beginning to form. "Commander J'ravi!" one man yelled.

Darien stepped forward to stand firmly before Garrick. "Perhaps you are right, my friend. Perhaps the city would be better off without you. Perhaps you are right to say Dorfort doesn't need you. But *I* need you, Garrick. And I need you now. I know what you can do, and I'll take my chances. I need you to go into my city and heal its wounded. They are innocents. They didn't deserve this."

Garrick raised his gaze to meet Darien's and saw the inner fire he had felt many months ago in Arderveer. His friend's gaze was firm and direct. It was personal.

"All right. I will do my best, though I don't know if you understand what you are asking."

"And the Freeborn?"

"Give them to Amanda. She is young, but she is strong and inventive. She'll hold the core together."

Darien nodded. "That is probably the wisest course."

"Whatever you do, it cannot be Reynard."

"I understand."

Behind them, the guard began to form.

"That's it, then," Darien said. "We have more to discuss, but first let's get Dorfort under some semblance of control."

"Agreed," Garrick said.

With that, Darien J'ravi, Commander of the Dorfort Guard, turned to take his post.

EXISTENCE

Braxidane knew the exact moment Hezarin died.

He'd been in his node, absorbing energy and considering whether to visit his future champion on the plane of Rastella. The youth there was the last of his champions, and was destined to become the most remarkable. She would grow in power as the rest grew in experience. When she was ready, Braxidane would make his play. He sipped at the power around him, and was letting the electric tingle of a pristine future unfold before him, when he felt the pulsing aftertaste of his sister's death.

A sense of pure disbelief came over him. Then one of absolute fear.

He flashed red with discontent. Then he gave a deep streak of purple resentment. His node became uncomfortably warm.

What had Hezarin done?

Why was she on Adruin to begin with?

It was only a matter of time now before All of Existence would learn of her death, and when that happened it would be only moments before Joint Authority would focus on her. They would discover her links, which would lead them to his links, which would then lead them to the rest of his champions. So, it was now only a matter of time before Joint Authority, and therefore All of Existence, would know what Garrick was capable of.

He let go of his connection to Adruin and dashed into the scouring flow.

This was going to be bad.

He had little time to lose.

NINETEEN

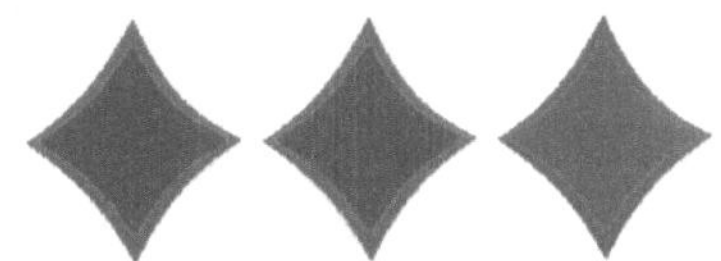

Garrick strode toward the gaping hole in the wall.

Once considered impenetrable by the public and by the leaders of this great city, its masonry was now broken and craggy. Its ironwork frames were rent and exposed, and its stone slabs were cracked open like eggs to reveal insides that gleamed with chalky brilliance against their weathered exteriors. Beyond that wall, he would find a city strewn with death and destruction, a city filled with people in need. He felt them already, bleeding, burning, crying out in the nighttime. The life force inside him yearned to be unleashed.

As he walked he thought three things.

First, that he was proud of Darien. His friend was a good man, battered and bruised, but a man who knew who he was.

Second, about Will.

And third, he thought about Braxidane and Hezarin, and All of Existence

He had felt his destiny while he was in Existence.

He had seen the future of the plane, and the future of all planes as long as they were open to the dalliances of the planewalkers. That thought twisted through him in ways worse than Braxidane's hunger ever could.

He belonged to Adruin. It had given him its energy. He had fed off its life force. Garrick felt the entire plane now as if it was under his skin, whole and vital and important. Perhaps, unlike Darien who yearned for the comfort of Dorfort, he had never felt completely attuned to any one place on Adruin because he belonged to the entirety of this world.

Perhaps.

But he knew one thing that no one else knew. He felt this place embedded deep in the power he held inside him now.

And he knew this, too: The people of Adruin would never be free as long as the planewalkers were free to use them as their playthings. These people who lie dead and dying would be alive and well now if it were not for Hezarin, and Hezarin would not have come here if it were not for Braxidane. What other machinations had combined to create this play? Garrick could not begin to guess. But he had seen All of Existence now. He understood that life there was a collection of shifting paths that lead to nowhere and everywhere at the same time.

He sighed then, feeling what he knew would not be the final shudder of Hezarin's life force.

The planewalkers would come for him.

That's what Braxidane had told him.

He thought about this as he came to the wall and surveyed the city proper.

"Fine," Garrick said out loud, crossing over the gates of the shattered wall that had once protected Dorfort's government center. "Let them come." He looked at the planewalker's devastation, then. Fully took it in. Watched as fires raged through the dark of nighttime to reveal wounded men and women who lay scattered across the open yard. They called to him with desperation. He felt each of them somewhere in the recesses of his mind.

The smell of burning buildings mixed with the blood-laced residue of Koradictine magic here.

Voices rang out, men calling for water brigades, and women giving orders as they pulled the injured from danger.

It was cold, the wind biting and blustery here in the open.

The people fought against the elements as well as the flames. Hooves clattered and pounded as horses and mules raced through Dorfort's rutted streets, taking wagons and men to places where they could best serve the fight. The whole of the city was working to save what they could, and he was glad to see members of the Torean Freeborn working alongside them to quell the flames.

But Garrick could not focus on these things.

Hezarin was gone—at least her body was nowhere to be found. Garrick had bested her. He had consumed her here in the manor yard of Ellesadil's government center. Her power remained behind, though, struggling against him, twisting and causing Garrick pain. He choked on the swell as it rose against his control. He concentrated on her, pressing her essence deeper inside him to where he could better staunch it.

Hezarin's life force pulled itself toward the injured, though, as certainly as it struggled to be free of him. The heat of flames warmed him as he stepped through the city. The sounds of panic pulled on him like the moon pulled the tides.

Their moans were low and pain-filled, their screams piercing. They gasped and they cried with despair-riddled callings—they were the city's guard and its common citizens, men and women who had taken up weapons against Neuma and then against Hezarin herself. They called through the night. Some pounded the ground beside them as they lay bleeding out their lifeblood before their very eyes. Some merely writhed in agony. But all of them stank of the same fear, the same anger, and the same despair. They made accusations (*What have you done?*) and clear calls to the Powers of Justice and Freedom and of All That Is Right. Their voices carried bitter, bile-filled screeds that demanded correction of whatever foulness had been done to them. Their pleas were laden with the demand that the hourglass be turned back, that things be returned to times that did not include whatever ruinous wounds had befallen them.

Help me! they called. *Heal me!*

Their screams brought Garrick memories of Sjesko, of Arderveer, and of God's Tower. He thought of the mobs of Rastella and of Karas-acti's prisoners. He remembered them all, even the first boy at the tavern where everything started.

And Arianna, of course. He remembered her, too.

There were rosters of them—hundreds of common people who paid the price of the planewalkers' frivolous games of court and double-jest. Thousands, he was sure, perhaps millions over the cast of time itself. The thought of such wanton disregard for life brought bile to his throat.

Something had to change.

Braxidane and the rest of the planewalkers had to be stopped.

The voices of the injured broke through to him again.

And Garrick, now filled past bursting with the planewalker's power, felt this yearning as if each calling branded his very core.

Power welled inside him, and he strode forward to flow life force into one man's torn limbs. The wounds closed, and Garrick felt the strength of the man's beating heart before he moved on. Next was a woman whose leg had been crushed, then a man—a shop keep by trade, but a man who had leapt to Dorfort's aid as Neuma rampaged, and had paid a price of fire. Garrick healed his burns, leaving barely a scar behind.

With each healing, the pull of desire from the masses became stronger, and with each of his touches, more voices came his way.

Garrick! they called. *I'm here! Heal me!*

He moved among them with such single-minded focus that time seemed to stand still. His touch released Hezarin's life force with a rush that tore at the sinew of his body. He bathed in the marvelous burn of giving, and he wallowed in a sensation of wonder as each of those he touched rose again. But with each rising, it seemed more voices came from the sea of pain that welled across the city. They came to him in masses that formed in the streets. They reached toward him, wanting to touch him, and him to touch them.

Hezarin's voice was husky at the back of his mind. *Do you feel the power, Garrick? You know you want it.*

Her voice broke his mindlessness. Yet still, he was filled with power and laced with yearning. Hezarin's purr felt like an engine inside him. He felt the touch of her fingernails come to his jawline, and he shuddered as she traced a path down his collarbone.

Yes, he thought to Heazrin's remainder as he strode through the city's injured. *Yes, I want it.*

Steeling himself, Garrick healed a man, then tried to wrest control of his magic back to himself.

There was a deeper thing here, an important truth he was forgetting. A truth that said the vacuum of this need was endless, and that even the vast energy of a planewalker would not be enough to save everyone. This thing inside him was cunning, though. It gave him his sway. It would let Garrick save the wounded and the dying until he was too drained to fight it, and then it would raise its dragon-vile head and enact its new price.

Actions and consequences, he could not help but think.

How terrifying would he be if he raged with the hunger left behind by a planewalker's void? In saving this city, Garrick could well destroy it. He touched a man and knit a broken arm, and power flowed also into another who pressed closer and grabbed his ankle.

He screamed, ripping his essence from the flow.

"No!" he said. "No!" he said again, and again, and again until he became fully conscious of himself.

Still he felt them, these people of Dorfort. They flocked to him like buzzards to a kill.

The power of the planewalker burned against his chest, and he sensed the unrelenting pressure of this wall of human need as he healed another, and another, and another.

He panted with desperation.

His muscles burned with exhaustion, and sweat flowed from his brow. His long hair became matted to his forehead and cheeks. His chest heaved with each breath as he felt the aftereffects of the planewalker's touch.

The gore-slimed hands of the injured still pawed at him.

They grabbed his shoulders and pulled at his torn sleeves, but he righted himself and he shook them away. Garrick had no way of knowing what the combination of Braxidane's magic and Hezarin's ambition would do to him, but he knew what it would do to Dorfort.

He had to leave.

He had to get away before he allowed them to drain him of Hezarin's energy.

"I will not give you what you want, Hezarin," he said aloud.

Her warped laugh echoed in his mind. *You don't know what I want.*

That was probably right, he thought. Hezarin was a planewalker, and planewalkers were devious animals by nature. This one had already duped Ettril Dor-Entfar and Neuma. *You don't know what I want*, was probably the most truthful thing he had ever heard a planewalker say.

"I know you want this plane," he answered. "And I know I won't give it to you."

Garrick put all his thoughts into the darkness of his hunger, following it once again to its origin, setting his gates, and mixing magestuff with the raw power of the planewalker's life force.

A hand clutched at his knee then slipped away.

A woman crawled onto his back.

He shrugged the woman away as he felt the connection open. All of Existence came to him through a shimmering doorway. He pictured a different place then, a place he had been before, and a place that might be available to him.

A place that might be safe, or at least a place that was not here.

And as more voices called his name, Garrick disappeared into the flow.

TWENTY

Darien looked at the manacled woman being held between two guards. Just what he needed. One night on the job, and what did he get?

A Lectodinian spy.

Marvelous.

While his city was falling apart around him, he paced before the spy, wanting nothing more than to beat her to a pulp. That was not who he was, though. That was not where he had come from.

Torchlight glowed from sconces that had been placed around the central meeting hall with mathematically precise spacing. They gave the ceiling a soft glow as its rounded shell rose above. A fresh crack ran down one curved side of that ceiling, a thin line that scored the masonry that was otherwise eggshell-smooth. Despite the torches, and despite the heavy skins his staff had placed over the windows— all of which had been shattered by Garrick's magic earlier—the chamber was cold.

Muffled voices came from outside. Darien wanted to be out there now. As Ellesadil's newly appointed commander, that's where he *should* be.

To make matters worse, the woman had taken great glee in giving him nothing of any value. Everything about her—the fiery glow of her cheeks, the razor-sharp glare of her gaze, the way she struggled against her manacles, and the way her voice bent as she used his title—spoke of contempt for him. She was clearly here on a mission, but nothing about that mission would be extracted from her lips without some intensified interrogations.

It all added up to make Darien angry.

"Take her to a cell," he said. "Stand a Freeborn apprentice as a guard, then return to your brigade and help get those fires out."

The guards turned to their tasks.

"You can't hide me away like this!" the woman wailed as the guards tugged at her manacled hands. "You know we're coming!" she yelled over her shoulder. "You are scum, Darien J'ravi! You are turds from the bowels of monkeys! When Zutrian finds me in chains he will not look kindly upon any of you!"

Then she was gone.

Darien raised an eyebrow as he scanned the rest of his captains.

They stood in awkward silence, uncertain of what Darien would do next.

"Such words to come from the mouth of a lady," he said.

The crew gave a nervous laugh, and Darien took a moment to examine the chamber. How many times had he met with the Freeborn here? How many arguments had he encountered standing on this very platform?

"I don't need to tell you what this means," Darien said. "If she's telling the truth, the Lectodinian order will know exactly what's happened within the day. And despite her lack of decorum, I see no reason to doubt her."

"And," Hinchley Ster, a sergeant of the North Guard added, "that means Zutrian will understand that the Koradictines are finished."

"Yes. That she was so adamant that Zutrian will come to Dorfort is troubling. Damage to the wall could take months to repair. The city is in no position to withstand a siege."

"Perhaps she was stretching the truth, sir," Hinchley responded.

"Perhaps," Darien replied. "Either way, we have more pressing issues to handle tonight. The Koradictine mage and her planewalker cut a blazing swath through the city. We have to bring it under control."

Darien turned to the map and gave instructions.

He put a detachment along each side of the path Neuma had taken, and he posted mages to the north where Hezarin's fires were blazing unabated. He wanted farmers to the east digging fire breaks to wall off the spread, and he wanted, more than anything else, to get Garrick to find a way to shut this whole thing down.

Where the blasted blazes *was* Garrick, anyway?

"Will?" he called, turning to find the boy striding down the darkened central hallway, his cape billowing behind him.

Darien waited for him to arrive, actually pleased to have a moment to do nothing but breathe.

Will entered the room.

The boy was still adolescently thin and only as tall as Darien's shoulder, but he had been through much in his few years. Will was becoming a man before his time. There was strength in the way his gaze connected to Darien's, and even though the boy's face was smooth and unblemished it carried a sense of confidence and action that was hard to ignore. Will had played a direct part in much of Garrick's activity and had lived to tell of it. Those experiences had changed him in ways Darien both appreciated and despaired of.

"Where is Garrick?" Darien asked.

"He is gone, Lord J'ravi."

"Gone?"

"Yes." Will set his jaw such that Darien knew the boy was as unhappy to report this as Darien was to hear it. "I watched him step into the void. That's why I came here. We need to do something about the wounded he was attending to."

Darien grimaced and turned sharply to the map. It was everything he could do to keep his composure. "Isn't that just like him to run away just when we need him most? And after he promised me he would help. After he promised me."

"He will return," Will said, squaring his shoulders defensively. "He always returns."

"But the city is burning *now*. And beyond that, it's clear that the Lectodinians will take advantage of this moment as rapidly as they can. I need him here, and I need him here now."

"The Lectodinians, sir?"

"Yes. They will soon hear of the Koradictines' fall and of Dorfort's inability to defend itself. Zutrian Esta will know the time is right for them to press their advantage."

"I see," Will said. "But I don't think you should plan on Garrick's return anytime soon, Lord J'ravi."

"You can call me Darien."

"I thought with your new title, sir."

"You are growing into a man, Will. And you are with Garrick. If you can survive beside him, I think it proper you call me by my name."

"Thank you ... Darien. But when Garrick leaves, it always seems to be for a purpose. I have found it best to assume he will be away for some time, though."

Darien examined Will closely. Yes, the boy was growing up.

"Can you find him? I know you've been dallying in magic yourself. Garrick has told me as much in the few quiet moments we've had together."

Will narrowed his eyes, contemplating. "No," he said.

Darien pursed his lips, contemplating his next step.

Will would not lie to him, but it would not be out of character to withhold information if he felt uncertain about it. And Garrick *had* told him that Will was pushing boundaries and pressing other Freeborn for ideas and hints. He was almost certainly finding ways to teach himself bits of magic wherever he could. It was likely Will had discovered more than he was letting on.

"You have a hunch, though?"

"Nothing real," Will said.

"You will tell me if you get such a sense that is more … real?"

"Yes, Lord J'ravi—Darien—I will."

"Good." Darien paused. "So, you were coming to address issues with the wounded?"

"Yes, I was. Garrick was dealing with them before he stepped away. Now they are calling out, and those that are able are gathering. If we don't arrange a medical center outside the walls, I don't think it will be long before they or their families begin to draw on Lord Ellesadil and his staff.

"I understand," Darien said, nodding. "And I'm sure you're right. Thank you. I'll attend to that at once."

He turned to leave, his thoughts already building.

The apothecary was certainly already out and working to save lives. He could reposition them, though it was probably wise now to have a detail stand guard for them.

"Darien?" Will said.

Darien stopped and turned back to Will.

"I want to be useful."

Darien smiled. "I can't imagine you would feel any other way."

"What can I do?"

"The stables," Darien said. "We'll need a steady supply of fresh horses around the city for the next full day. I can't think of anyone who will fit that role better. Tell the stable master I've assigned you to manage the process. Tell him your word is my direction. I need you to quell the horses, and ensure they regain strength as we shift them out to the city. Take care of them."

"Thank you, sir. I think I can do that."

"Then go and make yourself useful."

Will's face took a serious set, and he turned toward the stables.

Darien smiled as he made his way down the hallway. It was hard to be depressed for long when you were around a boy who was that … enthusiastic.

TWENTY-ONE

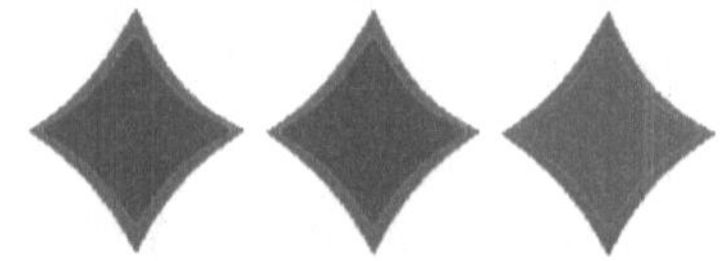

Zutrian Esta, High Superior of the Lectodinian order, had been enjoying the early morning darkness when the call arrived. It had snowed the day before, but the sky was a clear slate now—filled with pinpoint stars and a moon that was nearly full. His doeskin breeches and blue tunic were soft against his skin, and he sat on his open balcony encased by a sphere of power that kept him warm despite the altitude and the time of year.

Now, though, Zutrian's link sizzled with news of the most intriguing nature.

"The government center in Dorfort is in ruin," the ethereal voice reported. "By the time I arrived, Garrick had already disposed of the Koradictine."

"And what of Ellesadil?" Zutrian asked.

"The lord still lives, sir."

Zutrian grimaced, but despite that news he could still barely contain himself. His plan was working to perfection. His Lectodinian mages had spent the winter quietly picking off members of the already weakened Koradictines, and now, through a quirk of fate or luck, Garrick had disposed of Ettril Dor-Entfar. The Koradictines were, for all purposes, extinct.

His smile etched deep crevasses into his face. Life was beautiful after all. With Dorfort now needing to rebuild, this was the time. He was finally ready to take control of the plane.

"And there is something else, Lord Superior," the spy continued.

"Yes?"

"They say the Koradictine Garrick defeated was none other than Hezarin herself."

"Hezarin?" Zutrian said. "The planewalker? Not Ettril?"

"Yes, Lord Superior."

Zutrian paused. This story grew more intriguing with every breath. Hezarin, defeated by Garrick?

"Is there more?"

"No, Lord Superior. Not now. I'll stay in contact, though. There are bound to be ramifications."

"I am sure you are correct about that."

Zutrian broke the link. He sat under his magical shell and looked up at the moon that hung high in the sky. The wind howled outside his sphere, but he breathed only sweet mountain air. The discordance between the calmness of the moon and the rugged essence of the wind was apt, he thought. The moment had grown interesting.

Garrick, the Torean god-touched, was a wild card. That he could be powerful enough to defeat a planewalker was worrisome. Zutrian was aware that a rogue mage hunter had been on the prowl in the early months of winter and had assumed Garrick was the culprit. He had nothing to base that assumption on beyond his understanding of the Torean mind—he assumed that only a dogmatic adherent to their view of individualism would be wanton enough to go on such a spree—and the fact that whoever it was had been strong enough to defeat some good wizards. He couldn't think of anyone else who might be so inclined to pursue such a dangerous path, or gifted enough to survive it. Zutrian had considered dispatching mages to take care of the problem, but Garrick's pace kept him from being a major concern, and—to be quite honest—it was better to have him preoccupied with such vigilantism than focused on supporting the Torean House.

If Garrick were powerful enough to destroy a planewalker, though, he would need to be contained.

On the other hand, such news has ways of fitting its proper proportion with the distance of time, so he would wait for further reports before jumping to conclusions. And even if it were true that Garrick had destroyed Hezarin all by himself, her involvement at Dorfort would suggest that earlier reports of Ettril Dor-Entfar's death were also likely to be true. Elsewise, Dor-Entfar would have been there. And if *that* turned out to be the case, if Garrick had rid the world of both the planewalker *and* the Koradictine high superior, well ... then this was truly one of the more remarkable days in the history of his order.

He paused with satisfaction.

A thin cloud passed before the moon, bending its rays in a glorious act of diffusion. The rock was solid below him, firm and real. The foothills of the Vapor Peaks fell below, spreading from his balcony like a carpet blackened by shadow and lined with leafless trees, populated with bears in hibernation and birds of prey that searched endlessly for whatever scraps of food that carpet would offer.

It was a good land.

A fine place for a capitol, he thought, rubbing his sore knee and doing his best to ignore the toll the past year had taken on his body.

He needed to call his leadership council together to lay out the details of his plan. There would be logistics to cover and supply lines to put in place. The master plan had always been to approach Dorfort from three directions at once, so the order of battle had to include communications to ensure deception and timing.

There was much to do now.

Still, Zutrian was pleased enough that he found himself

humming a tune when footsteps fell upon the stone balcony behind him, and a gentle rap came at the doorway.

"Superior?"

The Lectodinian High Superior grimaced.

"What do you want?" he said, turning to begin his day.

EXISTENCE

Braxidane entered his brother's node without being invited. A social error, certainly, but Agar—posting himself so near to Adruin's gate as he often did—would be among the first to sense Hezarin's loss. He would be expecting Braxidane by now, and the others would not be far behind. To adhere to artificial amenities at a time like this seemed ridiculous.

"I want your help," he said as he took solid form against the node's wall.

Agar was braced against holds and was trailing filaments into the flow to draw energy. He pulsed with impatience. "When are you going to Joint Authority?" he replied, his voice soft, yet somehow still scouring.

"Why should I do that?"

"Surely you've considered throwing yourself at their mercy?"

"Are you suggesting I am guilty?"

Agar laughed a lemon-scented flow. "We are all guilty of something, Braxidane."

"Your point?"

"Maybe I have no point, brother. Maybe I have no point at all. But

I don't need to remind you that Hezarin had ties. She gave her word throughout All of Existence before going to Adruin. Now she is dead, and each of the lords she bargained with will be looking for someone to make good on those debts."

"So?"

"My guess is they'll expect her killer to provide for them."

"Garrick killed her," Braxidane argued.

"Don't jest with me. You, of all of us, know that we are responsible for the behavior of those we gift. And if I have my guess right, the problem you'll face next is that you won't be able to step into Hezarin's debt without exposing your other dalliances across the Thousand Worlds."

Braxidane became uncomfortably warm.

"What are you saying, Agar?"

"Unlike our sister, I am not a fool."

"I would never have called Hezarin a fool."

"But you would treat her as if she were one, wouldn't you? You would treat us all as if we were fools, really. Haven't you, after all, spread champions across the planes as if they were weeds?"

"How did you ..." Braxidane hesitated.

"I listen, Braxidane. And I ignore your sleight of hand and blustery conversation to focus on what you actually do."

"Sleight of hand?"

"Do you truly believe you can drop a tendril into every world you get even the slightest interest in without disturbing the flow? Did you actually think you could grow a fleet of champions without someone noticing? *Actions* and *consequences*, indeed, brother. Actions and consequences, indeed."

Braxidane condensed himself.

"Perhaps ..." he said, trying to find words.

But he stopped there, unable to carry on without actually voicing the full facts of his gambit. Everything had been moving along so well until now. He *had* been exploring several of the Thousand Worlds, and he *had* made champions in every one of them where he had been able to establish a presence. Garrick's case was just one example. He had found Garrick early and had pushed him in the right direction at the right times. But Garrick, unlike most denizens of the planes, was proving to be obstinate. He refused to play the game as it was meant to be played. Still, Braxidane wasn't going to admit everything to Agar if Agar wasn't actually aware of the *entire* depths of his game. His champions were growing older and stronger across the whole of the Thousand Worlds. In only a few short years, as measured on the planes, he would be strong enough to gain control of a majority of the gates across All of Existence.

When that happened, life as his brothers and sisters knew it would change.

But now Hezarin was dead, and, as Agar insinuated, things had become so much more than dangerous. Agar was also correct in his assessment of Hezarin's political foibles. There was every chance that her death, if not properly attributed, could result in a schism across the Lords of Existence that had not been seen for millennia.

Agar finally broke their silence.

"You do appear to need help, though, brother. Do you feel their approach?"

He did feel them. Their progress was a pressure across the media, which meant he had little time.

"I believe that means the Lords of Joint Authority have now learned of Hezarin's fate."

"What do you suggest?" he replied.

"Cut ties," Agar said. "Cast Garrick and the rest adrift. Leave all your champions to their own, and lie fallow for long enough that All of Existence forgets they exist."

"And if I do that?"

"Then I will back you, of course. I will block the other's motions when they petition Joint Authority themselves. I'll stall their argu-ments, and I'll argue that you are policing the situation properly. I'll offer to oversee your self-imposed sanctions. In other words, I'll give them an easy way out, but I'll be a pain in their side until they set you free."

Braxidane trailed cilia in the flow as he considered the offer. He chuckled sardonically.

He saw Agar's game now. He felt it. Tasted it in the essence of patience that rolled from his brother's node. He sensed the aroma of Zutrian and the rest of Agar's Lectodinian mages stationed throughout Adruin. And, now that he saw those patterns, he heard urgent whisperings in the flow. Preparations were being made, messages passed from Lectodinian lips to Lectodinian ears.

Braxidane's withdrawal would leave Adruin to Agar's influences, and it took only a few moments to sense similar situations among his other worlds. Agar had come along silently and set up camp behind him—a situation that could leave Agar in control of a majority of the worlds across All of Existence, the exact position Braxidane himself had planned to be in.

"You are cagey, brother," he said.

"Do we have an agreement?"

Braxidane considered his alternatives.

The sharp approach of the Lords built to excruciating levels in the flow.

"When I return, will I retain Adruin?"

"No," Agar replied. "When you return, you will have nothing but your life. But that is a start, isn't it? Certainly, it is something greater than Hezarin has now, and it is something greater than you will likely have if Joint Authority goes a different way."

Braxidane flashed red and orange.

It was an unpleasant position to be in, but it was as it was. He had to leave now or face the consequences.

The essence of the approaching Lords grew deeper.

"Yes, Agar," he finally said. "We have an agreement."

Then he dived into the gate that led to Adruin and left his brother alone to face the most powerful presence in All of Existence.

TWENTY-TWO

Garrick stepped into the desert, shivering despite his life force. It was dark here, just as it had been dark in Dorfort. The sky was crisp and the air cold.

It seemed that he had taken just a single step from Dorfort to Arderveer, as if his trip through Existence had been a simple passage through a doorway. He shook his head and splayed his fingers. He had felt the pull of Existence as he crossed through. The energy inside him yearned for the sea of life force he knew was there, and now the essence of the place danced over his skin like mist after a summer rain.

You are stronger than I thought you would be, Hezarin whispered.

"Perhaps you could have learned that from Braxidane," he replied despite himself.

Hezarin wasn't alive anymore, was she?

He wouldn't let her residual energy drive him insane.

She may have laughed then, or perhaps it was just the desert wind whipping through his hair.

Garrick sighed and lowered his head. He was tired of everything about planewalkers. Their constant meddling left him angry. No one could be truly free while any of these creatures held sway, and Garrick couldn't see any way to keep them at bay. He was a marked man, too. It wouldn't be long before the Lords of Existence would discover what he had done, and when that happened they would not leave him unpunished. There may be more to life than Braxidane's precious actions and consequences, but he was certain to pay a price for destroying Hezarin regardless of her provocation.

He stood alone in the desert, gazing over the flat plane of sand that he knew held the remains of a city below it.

Arderveer.

He recognized the feel of it.

Had it been nearly a year since he and Darien had made their trip to visit Takril? It seemed forever ago. He remembered Takril as a wild-eyed mage with a gemstone gaze and a bitter odor. He remembered slaves and desert knights. He remembered seeing mages of the two orders working together for the first time while in the city's underground hallways.

He decided on Arderveer because he knew he would be alone here. He wanted to think. He wanted to recover. And he needed time.

In fact, now that he had this moment alone he felt ...

He felt the whole of Adruin.

Yes.

Everything. All at once. The sensation was so strong it nearly choked him.

He felt Arderveer, of course. A few people still lived below in the fossilized shell of the city the orders had destroyed. Slaves who knew no other homes kept their places, and a pod of what remained of the desert knights appeared to be thriving. But there were gaps here, open places and caverns amid the city's destruction where he could retreat and take shelter while he sorted through his life.

This was good.

But he felt more than just Arderveer.

Even across this distance, he could feel the raw pain that still coated Dorfort. He felt its panic and the fear caused by flames that were eating its streets and alleys. The power of this panic brought a deep guilt that made him hate the planewalkers even more. To be able to ease this suffering, yet be forced to flee for fear of the devastation he could cause was debilitating.

And he felt more—people living, and scrounging, and working all across the plane, people taken with cold and fever, people growing strong. People tending bar, embracing, sleeping, and dreaming. People in Whitestone, and Farvane. People in the farthest southern reaches.

Hezarin's life force pulsed, and Garrick heard storms that pounded the Vapor Peaks. He sensed forests to the east as their trees dug roots against the winter, drawing nutrients through the soil and growing their footholds under the surface while—above—their bare branches seemed weak and brittle, and their trunks creaked under the pressures of a raving wind. He felt the moon above, rotating and raising the tide. He rode in ships on the oceans below that moon, their sails filling, their masts screaming against that same winter wind. The sailors were strong and firm against the salted cold, their heartbeats stout and bold. They were the best sailors, Garrick thought, the ones who worked this time of year—hearty and skilled, and able to look nature in the face and still sing their songs of joy despite ice so thick they would later pick it from their beards. He felt the owl that soared above the cliff faces to the south. He felt heat rise from the ground to create glassy waves of current others couldn't see.

Was this what every planewalker could feel?

No wonder Braxidane could be everywhere at once.

They were talking about you, Hezarin said.

"The Lectodinians?" he replied. He felt the power of that order in sentries who stood on a ridge along the Vapor Peaks.

No.

"I don't understand."

Yes, you do. You felt the truth only a moment ago. Try.

And, having now heard that statement put so explicitly, Garrick knew it was true.

He had heard the conversation as he passed through All of Existence. It had been there, so nearby he could have joined in if he had recognized it. But the flow had burned against his face for just that instant, and he had missed it. He was still digesting it all, though. The energy of that conversation was still twisting in his thoughts.

Cut the ties, someone said. *Leave all your champions alone ...* it seemed to come from the hairs that rose on the back of his hand.

It was not until he heard Braxidane's response (*and if I do that?*) that he understood what was happening.

"The Lords of Existence are coming," Garrick said.

That's right, Hezarin replied. *And your lord is giving you away.*

"He won't do that."

But he felt the truth in the bones of the conversation, and he felt other truths, too. He felt worlds upon worlds, and he felt men and women, people just like himself—champions each, and each tied to Braxidane just as he was. They existed, he thought. These other champions were as close to brothers and sisters as any he could imagine. And at that very moment, Garrick understood Braxidane would indeed give them all up if it meant saving his own skin.

Braxidane's voice echoed in his mind.

Yes, Agar. We have an agreement.

Inside him, Hezarin purred.

TWENTY-THREE

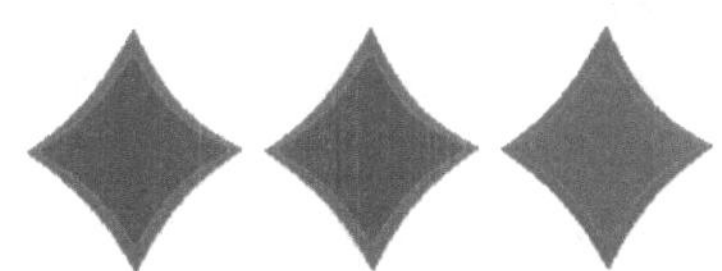

Braxidane would have had to come to Adruin soon enough, anyway.

For all his bluster, Agar's negotiations would almost certainly fail, and even if they didn't Braxidane couldn't stand to let Agar make a mess of something he had worked for so long to create. It was annoying, however, that his brother could use the pretense of protecting him to essentially banish him here. It was more than annoying. It was embarrassing. Knowing Agar had played him as a dupe was a slap to the face. Such disrespect could not stand.

He thought these things as he dove into the gate that led to Adruin.

Either the Lords of Existence would catch onto what Agar was doing early, in which case they would deal with him as they would, or Braxidane himself would have to go to Joint Authority to break Agar's play. Either way, the Lords would eventually come to Braxidane to extract justice for his own aggressions.

And that meant that, regardless of which path the future took, he would have to discard one champion to save the rest.

As Garrick was the least predictable of his mages, the choice was an easy one.

There was, however, a better idea than the one Agar had suggested—rather than destroy the mage outright, he would give Garrick exactly what he had been asking for, then let him flounder with the ramifications. This would at least give Joint Authority a true sense of where the incompetence sat in this arrangement. In addition, it might slow down the progress of Agar's Lectodinian partners. That possibility alone made the option worth pursuing.

So, however he looked at it, Adruin's proximity was fortuitous.

Needing a target to focus his arrival on, Braxidane felt for his champion as he flowed through Adruin's gate. He did not want to arrive directly in Dorfort, so he set himself down far enough away to take stock of the situation. Instead of being near Dorfort, though, Braxidane was surprised to find himself on the southern face of the mountain range that ringed the Desert of Dust.

He gazed out at the dusky horizon, seeing chromatic shades of heat that worked their way through the sands and misted into the atmosphere like dew over a morning swamp.

He wasn't sure what to make of this but thought it was good news on the whole. Being in Arderveer meant fewer distractions and a simpler extraction. At the same time, it seemed strange that Garrick was not in Dorfort. It said something had happened. Something had changed, and he didn't know what to prepare for.

It was all very intriguing.

It made him anxious, though he couldn't really tell why.

TWENTY-FOUR

Garrick worked his way into the underground chasms that had once been Arderveer. Feeling ghosts of the city flirt with him as he took each step, he descended broken stairways and traversed cracked passages. The caverns were dry and gritty. They reeked of the essence of the people who had lived here. Occasionally, he came across the presence of those who still made their homes in these caves, but he took pains to avoid them and they seemed to be unaware of his existence.

He liked that.

There was comfort in working alone.

He came, eventually, to Takril's central conjuring room, which he took as his own, sitting on the gem-encrusted throne that the insane mage had placed at the center of the chamber. Garrick left the area dark because he liked the sense of isolation it lent. He liked it because the darkness helped him focus on the field of energy that bled out of him now, radiating like heat from the sun. It was sitting in the still of this darkness that gave him to realize that those rays *were* his senses, that they stretched across the plane and touched everything that lived in ways that were both cold and intimate at the same time. It was this bleeding of energy that let him feel the world as it was. And here in the darkness, he knew something else, too.

It was changing him.

He thought differently now, reacted differently to everything around him. The power had seeped into him, and the combination of Braxidane's curse and Hezarin's power had made him into something new.

He thought about the planewalkers.

How did they go about their lives? Were they truly immortal? Did they have anything to do beyond toy with each other or play with the rest of the world around them? They were like children, he supposed. Like apprentices who were all grown up with nowhere to go.

He sat on Takril's cold throne and let himself relax.

His breathing slowed. His muscles went numb, and his senses rose.

His mind wandered.

As he sat on the edge of dream, his senses warped and he felt more distant connections. He sensed images of things beyond Adruin. Scents. Textures. He lived a moment of Hezarin's time with Neuma, then a moment of a distant plane. He followed the intense thread of current that flowed between the planes and felt grace in the casual swirls of its eddy pools. An interconnected sense of oneness came over him. The Thousand Worlds were beautiful in their way. The whole of creation was a being in itself, an organism that breathed and thrived together. Damage one, harm the rest.

And, amid this learning, he found a new thread, an interesting tie, a fresh truth about Braxidane.

The planewalker was ubiquitous. The print of his power touched everything, everywhere. He had other champions.

Of course he did.

Garrick felt foolish at first. He should have known he was just one of many. For a moment Garrick hated himself for having such hubris to think he might have been somehow special. But the simple fact was that Braxidane was using him, no differently than any other man of power used their subjects. And Braxidane was using the others, too.

He should have deduced that earlier.

His superior had always been an adroit liar.

Garrick stirred from his rest and opened his eyes in the dark quiet of the chamber.

Yes, he liked this sheltered pocket of air best of all. It was a place he could breathe, a place where he could draw strength from thinking, a place where he could plan.

That it also resembled a node in the middle of Existence did not occur to him.

Eventually, Garrick became aware of Braxidane's presence as it passed through the dark passages.

He supposed he should have been surprised. Yet he was not.

Garrick followed his struggles from afar as the planewalker progressed over similar paths as Garrick himself had picked through earlier. He did nothing to help his superior.

When Braxidane finally arrived at the throne room, he came forward in the form of a dragonfly, its wings beating phosphorescent rings of color into the pitch darkness of the chamber.

"What do you want?" Garrick said as he cast dim light across the chamber.

"Greetings to you, too," Braxidane replied as he took the human form Garrick had first seen him in—though he was perhaps taller this time, and thinner. Garrick found Braxidane's appearance awkward now, more comical than mystical.

When it became obvious Garrick was not responding, Braxidane continued.

"I bring you good news, Garrick."

Garrick raised a brow. "Tell on."

"I've come to offer you your freedom."

"Don't pretend with me, Braxidane. It does not sit well on you."

"What do you mean?"

"I know what you're doing. It won't work."

"I am merely here to give you the opportunity to be free of your curse—the very thing you have been pleading for me to do since the day we met."

"No, Braxidane. You are *merely* here to protect your own arse is what you are merely doing. Unless I miss my mark, you merely intend to go back on your word once again. Rather than lay low to ride out the damage you've created, you *merely* intend to remove whatever trigger you placed inside me, and then hand me to your Joint Authority, thereby attempting to prove to them that you are worthy of continuing to draw breath."

"That is not true," Braxidane said.

"It wouldn't be so bad if I was the only one you were trying to hang. But I'm of the expectation that you intend to provide this same opportunity to all of your champions across all the worlds—though perhaps you might just strip them of their power and hope the council will leave them alive. Of course, that means the others would *merely* be forced to live the rest of their lives without the aid of powers they've built those lives upon, lives that will then likely be short given the demands of the people around them."

"I would attempt to save them," Braxidane said, giving up any pretext. "Just as I would save you if I could."

"You disgust me," Garrick said.

Braxidane's magic rose.

Garrick braced himself and flowed thoughts toward the attack. Everything was so different now, so easy. Their magic clashed, and the chamber rang with an explosion that thrummed so deeply inside his chest that Garrick thought he might be sick.

Braxidane's next attacks were swift. Multiple slashes of sharp beams, a sickle that flashed past as Garrick deflected it, and a final all-encompassing blast that Garrick dealt with by capturing it in a shell of his own energy.

Then everything settled and Braxidane's heavy breathing was the only sound in the cavern.

"Is that it?" Garrick said.

"I don't want to kill you," Braxidane replied.

"How kind of you to leave that to the Lords."

"It is, isn't it? Perhaps I'm wrong, though." Braxidane smirked and stepped forward, readying a fresh barrage. "Perhaps the Lords would be just as happy with a corpse."

EXISTENCE

Agar took his position by edging his node gently toward the gate. He tried to stay between it and Leaxis—the acting Lord Council of Joint Authority—who was most definitely on her way. He did not want Leaxis to destroy the worlds he was so near to controlling. But, accompanied by her entourage, the Lord Council was in no mind to debate procedure.

"Greetings, siblings," Agar said to the collective as they halted before him.

"Where is Braxidane?" Leaxis replied.

The four others—Lar, Wadanti, Valpu-nof, and Idolfilane—stood beside her, each flaring power into over-bright shells they wove around themselves. Their tendrils trailed in the flow with charges that made it known that Leaxis was to be heard.

"He has been here," Agar replied. "But that was some time ago."

"You are aware he has killed."

"Certainly I am, Lord Council. But just as certainly you see the truth of the killing. It was not his fault."

"Tell that to Hezarin."

"Our sister was not without responsibility in this process. You cannot ignore that.

"Such details do not concern us."

"And, yet, they should. To destroy Braxidane for this would be to destroy a part of ourselves. Even you must admit that hurting yourself for no good reason is not prudent."

"Braxidane is a cancer. He must be removed. This decision is made, Agar, and you would be wise to stay out of our path."

"If our brother is such a cancer, why is it that, as we speak here in Existence, he is outside, toiling to bring his errant liege to justice?"

Leaxis hesitated.

"I'll tell you why," Agar continued. He stiffened his communication now, knowing it would be best to avoid deep inquiry at this time. "He wants to right this wrong. He wants to square events by being the one to bring his own champion to accountability. Which, I might say, sounds more than a little repentant to me."

Leaxis and her entourage shared considerations, and for a moment Agar thought he might have won the day.

"These things Braxidane is working on should not have to be set right," Leaxis finally said. "But we understand your position. It is not without merit. We will not destroy Braxidane as first planned. He will, instead, be banished."

Agar considered one more protest, but the Lord Council's demeanor was bold enough that he bit back on his words. While Joint Authority was slow and generally lenient toward the musings and conflicts of its constituents, it was also unyieldingly short-tempered when it came to dissent to its decisions.

"I see," he said. "How can I help you, Lord Council?"

Leaxis's aura faded to a golden red.

"Where is Braxidane?"

Agar drew on the flow. "He is in Adruin, Lord Council. As best I know, anyway."

"How convenient," Leaxis said.

She turned to her entourage.

Idolfilane flared green and cinnamon. Wadanti responded with a sense that tasted coarse and spicy, like a tomato fresh off the vine.

"Yes," Leaxis said, flashing a command. "I agree with both of you. Shutting him into that plane would be easiest."

On her word, the planewalkers moved to the Adruin gate and flowed great masses of energy through their bodies, warming the plasma trails around it and driving tight beams of its magic—its space-time mass, its radiation—into the gap that connected Adruin to the Thousand Worlds. When they were done, they returned to stand beside Leaxis in the central core of all Existence, leaving the portal smelted shut and pulsing with white-purple heat.

It would stay this way for a very long time. The capped gate would be a marker, a warning to other planewalkers who decided to stray from the path. There was no longer any connection between this plane and the Plane of Magic. No energy could get in, and none would get out.

Magic on Adruin was now doomed to the slow death of neglect.

Agar felt a roll of contentment filter through him. Wherever Braxidane was, he would no longer be able to access his powers.

This was good.

It meant Braxidane was out of his concern. Hezarin was gone for good. And—of more value at the moment—it meant Leaxis considered the situation to have been dealt with.

Agar could afford to wait the time of a reasonable cooling period, then use his own mages across the rest of the Thousand Worlds.

The wait would be worth it.

TWENTY-FIVE

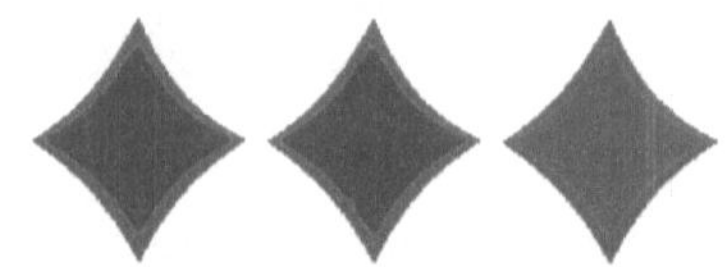

The blockage came as a rift in Garrick's consciousness. Where once there had been pressure, there was now a void. Braxidane paused in his spellwork with a gasp. His magic faded from his fingertips in Arderveer's dim chasm. He fell against a slab of rock, stunned. The expression on his face let Garrick know his superior felt it, too.

"What is it?" Garrick asked as he set his magic aside. But he knew the answer before Braxidane responded.

"They can't do this!" Braxidane said. "They can't."

And, yet, they had.

Garrick gazed upon Braxidane, the planewalker's fate dawning upon him. "You have been banished, haven't you?" Garrick said. "Joint Authority has sealed the plane."

"Yes," Braxidane managed despite panic that rolled off him in waves. "They have cut me adrift."

"They will seal the other worlds, too," Garrick said with bitterness that surprised him. He returned to Takril's throne chair. "They will cut off every champion you've ever created, won't they?"

"What is it to you?" Braxidane said, turning away.

"All of them will perish."

"I am sure Joint Authority will be bitterly disappointed if any live —including you, Garrick. *Specifically* including you. And yes, Agar, the lying ingrate, the despicable coward, will ensure Leaxis finds them all—while at the same time placing his own mages to fill the voids they leave behind."

Braxidane screamed then.

He pounded his fists against the wall, and the stone rumbled with such new stresses that, for a moment, Garrick feared a quake would entomb them both. Eventually, though, the planewalker's anger subsided and the ground stopped shaking.

"Including me?" Garrick finally said.

Braxidane's laugh was tinged with mirth.

"You destroyed one of their numbers."

"They have sealed the plane. Won't that be enough?"

"Of course not," Braxidane said, his throat raw and his voice ragged. "Search that power you carry within yourself and you'll know that Joint Authority will not leave you as a loose end. The sealed portal provides them time. It allows them to give you lower priority. But they will come for you in time."

Garrick contemplated Braxidane's words.

He felt the power of Braxidane's statement.

He understood.

Hezarin's energy would lead them to him.

Hers was an energy that should not be his. The lessons she learned filled him with things she understood and facts of her existence that no man of Adruin should ever have. They would stay with him, too, mixing with his own understandings to create new ideas. Garrick had turned into a creature stranger than any before, a man who was half human, half planewalker.

That made him dangerous to the Council.

It also made him unique. Different. It was a difference that would make him easy to find.

Braxidane gave what could have been a whimper. Garrick had

never seen his superior so pitiful before. It was not a becoming framework on him, though it seemed to fit quite naturally. "We are doomed," Braxidane said in a low tone. "We are *all* doomed."

"The whole plane?" Garrick said, catching Braxidane's meaning.

"Joint Authority doesn't do anything halfway."

"I see."

And what Garrick saw was how fragile his life could be, how fragile, indeed, all life across all the planes was when it was dependent on the benevolence of a few duplicitous creatures.

He thought about Darien, then. His friend had tried to teach Garrick the history of men throughout the plane's time, but Garrick had been tone-deaf. He had not listened even when the Shariaen had attacked them on their first trip together, but he still retained some stray pieces of Darien's stories.

"You're talking about Starshower," he said.

Braxidane leaned against the chamber wall and moaned. "What of it?"

"You're saying the Lords of Existence are going to unleash another Starshower?"

"What else would you expect?"

"Adruin will be left in shambles."

"We are all doomed." Braxidane slid down the wall to sit still, his elbows on his knees, his head in his hands.

"I can't believe Joint Authority will destroy the entire plane merely to get rid of me?"

"And me," Braxidane said, drawing a fateful sigh. "Don't forget about me. But don't waste time swooning for poor Adruin. It will rise again. These planes are like weeds that way. They always come back."

"I'm sure that will be a comfort to everyone here."

Garrick assessed Braxidane.

The planewalker was gaunt. He looked suddenly tired.

"You're an empty shell," Garrick said.

Braxidane looked at him through the dimness. He shrugged.

That shrug gave Garrick to understand a truth he had missed before. Braxidane, as all planewalkers were, was a shell that funneled energy. Now that he was no longer tied to Existence, he was defenseless. Garrick, on the other hand, stored energy within himself. His magic would last until he drained it—and then his hunger would ensure he recharged himself indefinitely, as long as people lived on Adruin. He shuddered at that thought and pushed it away to focus once more on Braxidane.

Actions and consequences.

Garrick could crush him.

A part of him yearned for that satisfaction, but Braxidane was to be pitied now and Garrick knew he could not do it.

"Go away, Braxidane," he finally said.

"Where should I go?"

"I don't care. But go as far away from me as you can. I have things to consider that no longer include you."

"You still have your magic, then?" Braxidane said.

"I am a different creature than you, Braxidane."

Garrick turned his lips down.

He wanted to think about Starshower. When would Joint Authority rain their power on the plane? Would it be based on a random decision, or would there be some logic applied? Would they perform the cleansing in such a manner as to give it symbolism? Did they care? Would they see their task as workmanlike, or would they bring an element of art to it? Whatever the answer to these questions, Garrick knew life on Adruin had changed. With the gate's capstone blocked, it would be only a matter of time before all standard magic died.

His heart froze.

That was when Starshower would come.

When all magic had seeped from the plane, the capstone would be lifted and the Lords of Existence would rain their catastrophe down upon the plane, thereby ridding it of all life—specifically including Braxidane and Garrick, the two creatures who could cause the Joint Authority the most damage.

He felt a deep sense of irony to this moment. Here he was, sitting amid the rubble in the depths of the broken city of Arderveer, contemplating the equivalent death and destruction of an entire plane of existence.

"I hope you are satisfied," Garrick said bitterly to Braxidane.

There was no response.

Braxidane was gone.

He nodded then. Good. He had better things to do than waste time on a deposed planewalker.

He sat for a long time and considered the world as he knew it.

He thought of the demise of the Koradictines and the destruction of Dorfort's defenses. He saw the opportunity this turn of events had left the Lectodinians. He felt the rising heat of Zutrian Esta's ambition as it rose from the Vapor Peaks and laid itself over Garrick's senses. He remembered Darien and his passion.

But mostly, he settled his mind on Sunathri Katella.

Lord of the Freeborn.

She had understood something deep and valuable about people. Garrick had traveled with and befriended Darien J'ravi, and he had grown to respect his friend beyond all doubt. But he realized now that it was Sunathri who had spoken to him. It was Sunathri's vision that most closely matched his own.

He rose from his contemplations prepared. He rose from them with an idea.

Adruin needed to band together to fight this—the Koradictines, the men of Dorfort and the plane itself, the Torean House of the Freeborn, and, yes, the Lectodinians. The people needed to band together if they were to survive.

Garrick knew where he had to start.

He had to speak to the Lectodinian high superior before Zutrian did something rash that destroyed all hope of a union with Dorfort.

TWENTY-SIX

The Lectodinian sentries were going about their preparations without any great anxiety, which told Garrick they were unaware of his presence on the other side of the rocky ridge. It was morning. There was breakfast to cook and tea to prepare. There were spells to set and traps to check.

Still, they should have noticed him.

It was cold here, made even colder by the altitude of the Vapor Peaks. Energy from the planewalker kept Garrick warm despite the simple shirts and thin cloth breeches he chose as his only adornments. His wardrobe would make a statement in itself here in the cold climes of the north.

His wardrobe, and his blades.

In that second category, he wore a pair of short swords, one at each side. And he enjoyed the feeling of the dagger he had strapped to one leg. The weapons made him feel purposeful. They were normal blades, a reminder of the simple nature of life. They gave him clarity.

Across the chasm, four sentries moved between tent-like structures of wood and skins. He caught the scent of the tea they were brewing over a nearly smokeless fire. The men were bored, their stoicism was like clay sediment at the bottom of his senses. It must be hell to be posted on a barren mountaintop for weeks at a time, waiting for nothing to happen.

He smiled. These sentries would soon have something to report.

He prepared his spellwork and steeled himself against a life force that rose like a tide inside him. Hezarin's energy was different from others he had consumed. She was a constant, a never-yielding thing. She was a presence full of prickly edges. And she spoke to him, too. She whispered things he did not want to know about places he did not want to be.

They are coming, she said to him in quiet moments. *My brothers and sisters are coming.*

She spoke to him of other things, too. She gave him the inner workings of the planes and the culture of the space between them, the space that *was* All of Existence. She told him of the pettiness between planewalkers, and showed him that they were not truly brothers and sisters but were best viewed as elements of a whole that fit together to make one single creature.

She was an actual piece of them. Her fellow planewalkers needed her. In learning this, he understood exactly how far they would be willing to go to retrieve her essence.

Garrick set his gates and focused on the Lectodinian sentries across the ridge.

His vision tunneled.

He tasted a caustic mixture of Lectodinian lemon and Koradic-tine blood as magic rose in his gut.

He spoke a word and twisted two fingers.

Then he was in their midst.

The closest Lectodinian, tall and wiry, emerged from a rickety lean-to. Time expanded. It was a feeling of ultimate power. As if he were encased in a shell—a node—that let him feel the raw edge of exactness everywhere. The Lectodinian seemed to move slowly. Garrick knew what the mages were doing before they did it. He felt calm and impervious, almost languid as he wrapped life force around the first mage's spell, then crushed it with barely an effort.

A bolt of life force flared from Garrick's outstretched fingertips, and the man fell like a sack. Another had been meditating but was roused by the blast. A twist of Garrick's hand put the man back to his slumber as the last two mages came out of the nearest tent.

One pulled a dagger from his belt. Garrick dropped him with a single motion, and the blade clattered against the cold, brittle stone.

It was so easy, he thought.

So easy.

The second mage pulled up short.

He was a thin man with matted hair that had likely not seen a cleaning for weeks. He wore heavy woolen pants, layers of tunics, and a poncho of animal leather that was probably boar skin, but was stained and dirtied past recognition. His gaze wavered. His eyes grew wide. His brow rose in dual arches.

"You're the god-touched?" he said.

"That is what some call me."

"What do you want with us?"

Garrick smiled. "I want an audience with Zutrian Esta."

"The High Superior?"

"Yes."

A gap-toothed grin crawled across the Lectodinian's face. "Is that all? I mean, might I interest you in Lord Zutrian's stash of emeralds while I'm at it? I'm sure I have as much chance of nabbing them as I do an audience."

"No, thank you. An audience will be quite enough."

Garrick waited while the mage took in the situation.

"I mean it," he finally said. "Get your gear on. I want to speak with Zutrian in person and I don't know where he is. But you do. Or at least you know how to get me to a place where someone will. So you are going to take me to that place."

"What about these men?" He pointed at his compatriots.

"Those who still live will be fine."

The situation traveled over the man's expression. He glanced to his tent.

"Let me get my boots and my breakfast."

"Get your boots," Garrick motioned his acceptance. "You can gnaw on breakfast as we walk."

The man nodded, realizing it was as good as he could hope for. He gathered his worn footwear from the tent.

"I don't understand," the mage said as he slid a boot over one foot. "If you are Garrick, the god-touched, why not just trace your way to Zutrian? Cast a spell. You could do it, right?"

"Yes," Garrick said. "I could."

The man slid on his second boot.

"So, why do it this way?"

Garrick paused. He could certainly have contacted Zutrian directly through the magical constructs Sunathri had taught him. In truth, Hezarin's energy made that magic even more straightforward to perform. But he didn't want to waste energy if he could help it, and beyond that, Garrick had learned enough to know better than to give a politician time to think. Holding such a conversation remotely would give Zutrian the ability to avoid him, or worse, prepare for their meeting. He wanted this discussion to be direct and firm, and he wanted a decision on the spot.

"I guess I'm just here to make your life more difficult," Garrick finally said.

The man grimaced as he tested the fit of his boots.

"Then you're doing a fine job of it," he said.

"Are you ready?" Garrick asked.

"Ready as ever."

"Then, lead on."

TWENTY-SEVEN

As he left Garrick behind, Braxidane knew he had to get off this plane. The passage he found had been a stairwell at one point but was damaged in the fighting. He fought his way up it, wriggling through tiny spaces left by crumbling rock. It was hard, painful work, but without his link, he had no alternative. Sweat poured from him as he pulled himself out of the crevasse to lie gasping upon a rocky ledge that looked out over the Desert of Dust. His clothes were dirty and torn, his fingers scraped and bloodied. He could not remember hurting so badly in all of his consciousness.

Agar was going to pay for this.

He lay baking in the sun on a dais of wind-worn sandstone, and held a hand up weakly to shield his eyes from the sun's blazing orb. It helped for a moment. Blinking, he saw the desert lie brown and dry to his north and west, and that mountains rose to his south and east.

His stomach grumbled. He was hungry. It was an embarrassment to feel such crude human needs. And, now that he was settling in, he realized his odor was something atrocious. Why him? Braxidane thought. Why not Agar, instead? Why was he punished like this when his underhanded brother was allowed to retain his power? He could not live like this. He would not live like this.

He wanted his connection back.

There were ways to make it happen, too—seams in the Thousand Worlds that could be accessed. But they each took power. He had no idea where he might find that kind of leverage on this plane beyond Garrick, and he knew better than to expect his champion would help him now.

He would find a way, though. He had to.

When he did he would return to Existence and take his revenge on Agar and on the whole of Joint Authority. It would serve them right. No planewalker deserved to be cut from the world like this. Ever.

Braxidane pulled himself to his hands and knees. The sun felt better against his neck than it did on his eyes.

Dorfort, he thought. The Freeborn.

Garrick may be of no service, but the mage had stationed his Freeborn House in Dorfort along with his human friend.

Darien. That was his name. Yes, Darien.

Braxidane was still a planewalker to some. If he could find the Freeborn, he could get some help. Darien was a human who might be able to make such a connection.

Yes. That was the plan.

Merely having an agenda gave Braxidane the strength to stand and the strength to walk, and even the strength to pull a few weeds and trap a lizard for a disgustingly raw meal. By the time the sun had disappeared, he was feeling almost normal.

Whatever normal was, anyway.

He traveled that night, setting his course eastward, thinking about Dorfort City, and thinking about how he might best address the one named Darien.

TWENTY-EIGHT

Zutrian watched his commanders from the comfort of his observation nook. They sat around his table, muttering, laughing, and conversing in animated tones, waving their hands as they told their tales. Goblets, each drunk to low levels, sat before them all, and each having been drained more than once before. He wanted to see how each of his staff was reacting to news that the Koradictine order had been destroyed, and to the issues caused by the sudden restriction of the flow of magic through their gates.

What he saw did not surprise him.

The ambitious ones, leaders like Kartha and Halsten, moved through the collective before the meal, shaking hands and pretending to listen to the others, but they finished each conversation with exhortations that supported their own further efforts. Others seemed to merely be pleased to have something to celebrate. They spent most of the session smiling and calling for toasts as their cheeks became ruddy with the drink. Still others were quiet and reserved—perhaps more content to be patient.

Cara was one of those.

She sat alone for most of the dinner, eating with a relaxed confidence that said she knew the entire meal would be eaten before anything of concern would be addressed. She savored each mouthful before moving on to the next. Cara had only recently returned from the banishment she had received as a result of her failure at Arderveer. Though Zutrian didn't know what she had seen during her time on the dark, gritty plane of Castagar, he knew it would not have been pleasant. Cara carried that experience within, though. She had not spoken of it upon her return and he was not inclined to ask until she was ready to share. All he could say with certainty was that Cara's eyes were colder than when she had left and that she sported a scar that ran from the side of her jaw bone, and down her neck, to eventually disappear under the collar of her robe.

And he knew this, too: whatever tasks she commanded in the future would be executed with precision and efficiency.

When the dinner was completed, Zutrian stepped through the curtains that draped the back wall. He wore a silk tunic of the darkest blue, and a pair of leather breeches oiled and buffed to a shine. Silver chains hung from his neck, and rings glittered from his dry and bony fingers. A triangular tattoo was easily seen on the back of his left hand, which he kept strategically exposed as he crossed his arms. He wore a long cape lined with wolf fur that fell from his shoulders nearly to the floor.

Silence settled.

Zutrian may be an old man, but he was still lithe, his muscles still firm and strong. The order buzzed with rumors of their Superior's daily physical regimen, and he cut a sharp figure in support of those stories.

"My commanders," he said to the collective. "We have driven the Koradictine order to the brink of its extinction. Congratulations on this outstanding performance."

The room shook with a throaty roar.

"Over the brink!" Halsten yelled, raising his goblet.

Another roar filled the chamber.

Zutrian smiled, an expression that was more a simple pulling back of his lips than a hearty, all-out grin. Success had been a scarce commodity this past year, and he didn't want to dampen his order's enthusiasm while it raged.

"On to Dorfort!" Halsten added when the clamor subsided.

This time the roar was not so throaty.

Zutrian held his palms down and waited for the cheering to fade.

"We are right to celebrate," he finally said as the mages quieted. "It is good that the Koradictine order is gone from this side of the map. But the plan is laid out, and we've each agreed to it. As heady as our victory has been, we will not outrun our chargers while the winter rages."

The gathering settled.

"And what of the links?" a voice called. "What of the plane of magic?"

Zutrian nodded.

"That, too, is an issue we must examine before we enact our plans."

"It is the same for all mages," Halsten said, his voice sloppy with drink. "And we have enough power stored in potions and catalysts and crystals, regardless. No other mages will be stronger. It is wisest to strike now—while the inability to retrieve power from Talin ensures our invincibility."

Zutrian replied with a touch of spite. "We will move quickly, Halsten, but I see no reason to rush this. Our plan has been exceptional, so far. We will spend the next few weeks recovering from our efforts, then we will move forward."

"But we have the advantage now," Halsten said. "We should take Dorfort while we have the chance. And we should drive west to finish the Koradictines off for good."

A few heads nodded.

Zutrian stepped to Halsten's side of the table.

"Indeed, we do have the advantage today. And we'll continue to have this advantage for the near future. There is more to this than

Dorfort, though. We will need to take Whitestone, and Badwall, and Spire if we are to control the plane. This is the time for final preparation, for building our strength, and then, come the earliest thaw, for positioning our forces such that we can unveil the final chapters of our plan."

Halsten sat back with an unpleasant scowl on his face, as—Zutrian noted—did Kartha.

"So celebrate today," Zutrian added, turning back to the gathering as a whole. "Sleep late and recover tomorrow. I'll expect you each to report to this very room the following day to prepare for the next wave."

A cheer rose.

Goblets chimed as toasts were consummated.

Zutrian watched the gathering, noting that Cara merely chewed on a roll.

This exchange had been useful in more ways than one, he thought. Then he left again, stepping back through the heavy drapes to give his commanders the opportunity to speak among themselves.

It was then that the runner came to him.

She was a child, perhaps nine or ten seasons old.

"What is it?" he asked, handing his cloak to his maid-servant and striding down the hallway toward his chambers. It was growing late and he needed his rest.

The runner scrambled to keep up with him.

"I'm asked to tell you that you have a visitor, Lord Superior."

"I do not wish to see anyone."

"Yes, Lord," the girl said. "I understand, but I'm told to explain that the visitor is a gentleman named Garrick."

Zutrian stopped so abruptly the runner found herself ahead of him. She stopped and returned to his side, her face showing fear that she may have been too forward in racing so far before the lord.

"The Torean?" Zutrian said.

"That's correct, Lord Superior."

"And no one else? He is alone?"

"I understand Garrick is escorted by a sentry from the peaks, Lord."

Zutrian's eyes widened as he grasped this most remarkable news. He ran his hand over his chin. Why would Garrick be here? Was he really this foolish? Who in their right mind would march into the den of his enemy all by themselves?

"I am told he wants an audience," the runner said, twisting her foot awkwardly, obviously uncertain of what to do next.

"I understand," Zutrian said. "Ask the guard to take Garrick to the ceremonial hallway. I will meet him there."

TWENTY-NINE

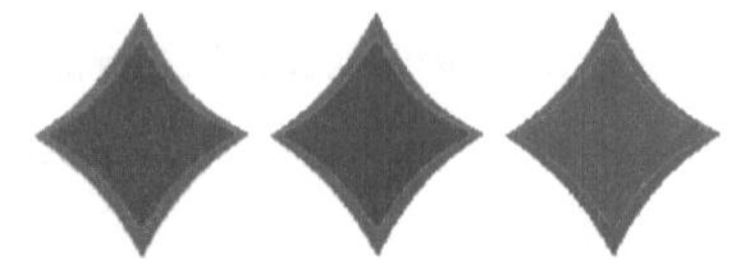

Flanked by four Lectodinian guards, Garrick stepped into the chamber.

It was a rounded cave, carved from the granite center of the mountain itself and polished to a shine. The air here glowed of the purple-tinged magelight that came from sconces cut into the walls. The ceiling was high, with a surface cut in faceted angles that had been made mirror-smooth. Those facets formed the light into beams that encircled the dais whereupon the throne sat, and whereupon that throne sat Zutrian Esta, High Superior of the Lectodinian order, swathed in robes that blazed blue.

Mages ringed the room, surrounding Garrick.

The full aura of Lectodinian power thrummed as if it came from the bedrock itself.

This was a powerful room, a room that could have many uses.

"To what do I owe this honor?" Lord Esta said from his perch.

He was dressed the part of his role, crisp in his robes and covered in a skullcap that gave him a strident look. His arms rested comfortably on the throne, which was made of rock and was padded with blue pillows fringed with golden thread.

"I come to discuss the whole of Adruin," Garrick replied.

"A worthy topic."

Silence permeated the room as Esta stared dispassionately at Garrick.

"I expect you have plans to take the plane when springtime comes," Garrick said. "But I have news that may cause you to rethink those plans."

"And that news would be?"

"You are aware that the gate to the Talin is now closed?"

Zutrian's face gave away nothing, but the slight hesitation in his response told Garrick all he needed to know. Zutrian was both aware of the blockage, and more worried about it than he would let on before his constituency.

"Why might this cause us to amend any of our plans?"

"You understand that the gate is closed forever?"

"That remains to be seen."

"No, Zutrian. It does not remain to be seen. This will not go away. The planewalkers have closed the gates, and there will be no more magestuff beyond what you have stored."

"Luckily, then," Zutrian smiled, "we have a not inconsiderable supply."

"Is that the best answer you have? Do you understand what this means?"

Zutrian sat calmly, holding this phlegmatic composure as heat rose in Garrick's face.

"Why did you come here, Garrick?"

"I want to make an arrangement with you."

"And why would I do that?"

"Because the water is even deeper than you worry it might be. The planewalkers will not stop at blocking the flow of mage stuff. They will not leave us to our own."

"And for that we should make an arrangement with you, because...?"

"If we do not find a way to fight this together, there will be another Starshower. Then we will all perish."

Zutrian's laugh echoed in the enclosed chamber, then the room became silent.

"Canado?" Zutrian said, turning his head to the mage at his left.

"Yes, Lord Superior?"

"Let me ask you a question."

"As you would, Lord Superior."

"Do you find the timing of our guest's news to be rather odd?"

The mage pursed his lips. "Certainly, Lord Superior. I do."

"How so?"

"He comes from Dorfort."

"Yes. He does. And why is that a problem?"

"The city is in shambles, Lord Superior. I'm certain its leaders expect an attack at any moment."

"You think so?"

"They are not unwise, Lord Superior."

"No," Zutrian said, turning back to Garrick. "They are not unwise."

Garrick narrowed his gaze. "The people of Dorfort don't even know I am here, Lord Esta."

Zutrian laughed again, this time harder than before. "That is another very good one, Garrick, God-touched of the Toreans and friend of Ellesadil. You have not failed to entertain us this evening. That much is true."

He spoke to his mage again without lifting his gaze from Garrick's eye.

"Canado?" he said.

"Yes, Lord Superior?"

"I believe your analysis is well-made. And given these turns of events, I would like you to inform the council that we will be moving our activation date forward. Please pass this news along. You may leave now."

"Yes, Lord Superior."

The mage left the chamber through a side exit.

Garrick had failed. His trip had been for naught. Zutrian was an imbecile, no different than any other politician with power, no different from any other man who was blinded to the truth by an agenda he had already defined. Zutrian would not be swayed. He would not join forces with Dorfort.

Garrick bowed his head slightly.

"Shall I assume you will grant me my leave as peacefully as I arrived?"

"That is only proper, Garrick. Lectodinians are not barbaric. But next time we meet, do not assume we will be as civil."

"I understand, Lord Superior," Garrick said.

Then he left the chamber.

Once he was outside Zutrian's stronghold, he transported himself back to Arderveer, back to his dark throne room to ponder the situation. It cost him a touch of his remaining energy, but the time he saved was worth it.

He would have to find another way.

THIRTY

Darien had barely slept over the past three nights. The Lectodinians were coming. There would be time to sleep when the wall had been rebuilt.

This morning he stood on the edge of the shattered front gate and watched as masons spread mortar and set stone. It was a warm day, finally. A portent of spring to come. The wind blew his hair back and carried the scent of lake and woods. It was good to get up here on what remained of the wall, up here away from the muck and mire on the ground.

He gazed to the north, then to the west.

No signs of a raiding force, yet.

Pleased, Darien turned his attention to three smiths who had set up nearby forges and were working to smelt iron girders that would fortify the new wall. He had overseen the design himself. They would hold. At least, they would hold if they were finished in time.

"Darien?"

He turned to find Will standing beside him. The boy seemed to be growing taller every minute.

"Good morning, Will."

"Are you avoiding me?"

"Why would you ask that?"

"Because I've been requesting time with you for two days, yet you have not answered."

Darien waved away the accusation but knew there was truth to it. Will reminded him of Garrick, and every time he saw the young man he felt anger. Garrick was too fickle, too strange. He could not be counted on. Garrick was a man who ran from problems rather than faced them straight on, a man who let his fellow citizens down when they needed him most. Darien blamed himself for his anger, though. He blamed himself for imagining it might have been otherwise, for thinking Garrick would change as he grew a truer understanding of the world. Men like Garrick were selfish. They worked to a rhythm of their own making. Men like Garrick did not change.

"This is a very busy time, Will."

"That's what I need to talk to you about."

"Tell on."

"I want to join your guard."

"I don't think Garrick would approve."

"I am not a child, Darien. Not anymore. And I know the Lecto-dinians will be coming. Garrick will be upset that I joined your ranks, but I am not yet a mage, and I can't see any other way to do my part."

Darien smiled.

"I like your fervor, Will. Garrick would be wise to emulate it."

"So where can I help?"

"The stables—"

"I've done my part with the stables, Darien. I want to do more. I want to fight."

Darien glanced north again. He rubbed weariness out of his eyes with the back of his hand.

"I don't think that would be wise," he said.

"I know how to handle a weapon."

"I know you do. But a battlefield is no place for a man as young as you are."

"And I know magic, too. Some, anyway. I was teaching myself more every day until everything shut down."

Darien chuckled. "As only a Torean should."

Will leaned backward and took in Darien as a farmer might assess a prize steer. "I see it now," he said. "You're afraid of Garrick, aren't you?"

"Garrick is not here," Darien said, unable to keep spite from his voice.

"But you know he will return, and you're afraid that if he comes back to find I've taken up a blade, he will hold you responsible."

Darien crossed his arms and took a defensive breath.

"It doesn't matter, Will. You're not going to be in the Dorfort guard, and that's final."

Will frowned. His gaze bore holes into the back of Darien's head.

"I'll find a way," Will said, his face growing stern. "You can't stop me."

Darien's temples pounded even deeper, but he found himself appreciating the boy more. It had already been a long day. But standing here on the wall, with the soon-to-be spring air flowing through his hair, Darien understood why Garrick liked the boy. It was hard not to be drawn to the way Will saw through to the core of a situation, and how he focused his energy in places that mattered. Darien laughed. It felt good to laugh, actually. It was the first time he had done so with such sincerity since arriving back in the city.

"I'm sorry to laugh, Will. But we do need you in the stables right now, so I would like you to go there. I look forward to speaking of your future later, though."

Will turned and fled the wall, but not before his cheeks reddened and his eyes grew wet.

THIRTY-ONE

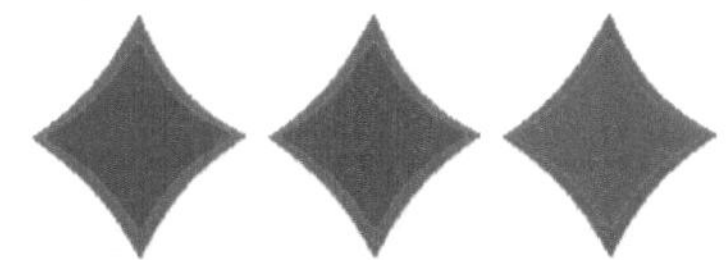

Garrick was back in Arderveer, stewing on the hundred ways he wanted to harm Zutrian Esta and Braxidane when the idea struck him.

He needed to find one of Braxidane's other champions.

It was, admittedly, a ridiculously far-fetched idea. It was an idea that had no chance of success for the simple reason that the problem that kept him from making it happen—the blockade of Adruin from the rest of Existence—was the same problem he needed the champions' help to solve.

Unfortunately, it was the only idea he could muster.

The Lectodinians were not going to help. The Koradictines were no longer of any power. Darien and Ellesadil were too focused on Dorfort to listen to issues on the scale of All of Existence, and the planewalkers themselves were the actual problems. That left only one other group with enough power to help and enough stake in the game that they would consider doing so.

So, yes. He needed to find one of Braxidane's other champions.

Better yet, he needed to find *all* of Braxidane's other champions.

Then he needed to bring those champions to bear on the Lords of

Existence. It was the only way to stop the planewalkers from toying with the planes whenever their bickering seemed to call for it. Nothing would make him happier than to stop these "gods" from destroying the lives of countless people who were simply living their innocent and otherwise oblivious lives.

The circular nature of the situation made it impossible, though.

He needed to break the seal on his plane to get to the other champions, and he needed the other champions in order to break the seal on his plane.

It all added up to the fact that Adruin was doomed.

Sitting alone in Arderveer's darkness, Garrick felt the weight of that doom draped across his shoulders as if it were a water-logged bearskin. He sensed the ebb and tide of energy as it settled into stasis across the plane. It molded against his mind like the liquid in a water skin, shifting and sliding. It filled empty cracks in the cosmos of the plane's being with its slippery breath, but it no longer had current. It no longer flowed. It reminded him of life before he had been touched by Braxidane. Warm, yet insubstantial—cold, yet somehow so tantalizing he could not imagine being without it.

The plane's barrier was that water skin. It held the power of all of Adruin inside it, constraining it, limiting it, holding it together like his own skin held together his innards. It made him morose to think that someday all those innards would drain away. Not immediately, of course, but someday, over time, slowly, certainly everything about him would fade away. That was life. Or, as Braxidane would say, the long fade to death was the consequence of life. And as long as the gate was cap-stoned, Adruin's end game was foretold.

It was then that the rest of his idea formed.

It came in layers, congealing so slowly that he wasn't exactly certain when it had arrived, or indeed if it hadn't been there all the time and merely needed to be uncovered. But it came together in a moment when he was thinking about Will, and about how boundless the boy's future should have been. He was remembering Will's optimism and how it seemed to leak out of him like some kind of fresh-scented perspiration, and yet how Will never seemed to run out of it.

And the idea hit him.

Where would the energy go?

If Adruin was to be depleted of its life force, but its path to All of Existence was blocked, where would it all go?

And, more importantly, and more relevant to the moment, if all of Adruin's life force and all of its magical power were to be drained, how would it leave?

The question brought him upright.

He remembered Braxidane's comment.

"Don't waste time swooning for poor Adruin." Braxidane had said. *"It will rise again. These planes are like weeds that way. They always come back."*

He asked himself: If lands in capped planes rise again, where does the life force come from?

And he knew the answer.

There had to be other passages. Other flows.

Leakages, maybe.

If the plane's barrier was a water skin, could it be breached elsewhere?

As soon as he thought of it in this fashion Garrick sensed a change, a permutation in the flow that was so tiny as to be impossible to feel without looking for it. Miniscule portions of power slipped out of the bladder that held it.

And then what?

Evaporated away? Disappeared?

Flowed into something bigger outside the plane? Into Existence itself?

Maybe.

But if he was right, that seepage would work both ways. Once the plane of Adruin had been drained of its life, its empty husk would lie like detritus in the flow of All of Existence and then it would soak up energy in this same slow fashion, life force slipping in through the very walls of the world itself.

Could he use this?

Garrick set gates and concentrated on the points of Adruin where he sensed the outflow. He wrapped Hezarin's energy around himself. A space opened before him—a bubble, or a seam in the construction of the plane. Garrick followed that hole and steadied himself as he tottered on the seam it exposed. It was warm here, lit with faded orange and green glowing that made everything feel disjointed and out of place. He stepped his way along the seam. As he moved, a hum of power made his stomach churn. The hairs on his arms rose. The air smelled of overripe fruit.

He knelt and ran his hand along the seam.

Existence. Yes. It smelled of the place.

Without thinking, Garrick funneled more magic through his gates. He grabbed handfuls of his own life force and stuffed it into his spellwork. Then he slipped his hand firmly into the seam. He pried at it with vigor, pulling more energy around him to create the shield he knew he would need.

Soon the gap was large enough for him to slip through.

He recognized All of Existence as he would recognize anything that was a home. That part of him that was Hezarin expanded toward the energy as if it were hunger itself. Panic gripped him as he watched his fingers extend to become wafting tendrils. He choked as they wriggled out of the protection of his shell to trail in the energy that was Existence.

Pleasure shuddered over his entire body.

He breathed that pleasure in, and when that breathing reached its full extent he breathed deeper still, reveling in the excruciating release that stretched his lungs.

Yes.

He was a changed man now. He didn't need the shell.

His tendrils glowed golden. Energy coursed through him with a rhythm that felt like the beat of a heart. He felt everything around him as if it all lay just under his skin. The limitless expanse of the universe made him dizzy.

Was he now a Lord of Existence?

Hezarin laughed at him in the deep recesses of his mind.

No, fool. You cannot be one of us.

He believed her, but if he was not a planewalker, then what was he?

He stretched out his cilia and tasted the energy's cinnamon burn.

Braxidane's essence remained in the flow. He felt each place where Braxidane had built a node. He felt his superior's links as if they were a map—as if they were passages that led to Braxidane's planes—clear and simple, easy to follow. A line tied him to Braxidane, and hundreds more tied him to each one of Braxidane's champions across the Thousand Worlds.

They were exactly what he was looking for.

He turned to follow the first link.

THIRTY-TWO

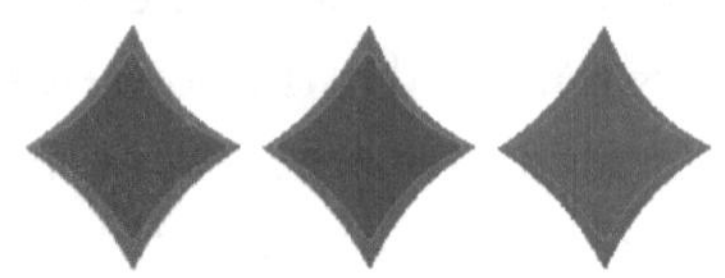

Will stepped quietly to the alcove outside Darien's war council.

Being silent and unobserved was a skill he had learned well over the past year, having often slipped through the government center's hallways to listen when Darien's father had briefed Lord Ellesadil of news related to the clash at God's Tower. The building was rife with passages a boy known for being precocious could get lost in. Now he used them to investigate tales of a strange visitor who had arrived in the city during the late hours of the night, demanding that the guard let him see Darien.

Will knelt to one knee and pressed his ear to the door.

He heard a strange voice.

"If you do not help me, your city will burn whether you defeat your Lectodinian horde, or not," the voice said.

It took Will a moment to place it.

Braxidane.

He nearly yelped at the realization. The visitor was Garrick's superior.

"Let me see if I have you correctly," Darien said. "You are saying that these planewalkers, the Lords of Existence, have cut off the flow of magic to Adruin."

"That is what I am saying."

"And you are also saying that they intend to unleash a new Starshower that will ravish the plane?"

"That is also correct."

"That makes no sense."

"It makes perfect sense. The lords locked the plane to punish me, and perhaps to punish Garrick. But, in the end, they will destroy Adruin merely to make an example of him. Of that you should have no doubt."

Will grimaced. He had never liked Garrick's high superior, but he knew it was true that the gates had been shut. Complaints from the Freeborn and the failure of his own attempts to practice spells had told him that. But while that part of Braxidane's story held up, Will didn't trust the planewalker as far as he could throw a mare. He would bet anything that there was more to this than Braxidane was telling, and it took every bit of his self-control to *not* burst through the door and hurl an accusation at him.

"What do you think of this, Amanda?"

Will listened more closely to catch the softer strain of Amanda's words.

She was young, but after Garrick's disappearance and Reynard's treachery, she had taken responsibility for the Torean Freeborn and had been able to hold them together with some acumen. Will was interested to hear her position.

"Access to the plane of magic is definitely closed. That hinders all magic, and will obviously slow the Lectodinian's efforts. But I'm sure Zutrian's mages have sources of stored power. If anything, the blockage might accelerate his plans. He could decide to engage before the Lectodinian stores fade further and he loses that advantage."

Darien spoke then.

"So if we can delay them, fight them here," the thump of a hand against a wall or table gave Will to imagine Darien indicating a map, "and here," another thump, "and maybe even here, they will be less able to damage the city?"

There was a pause before Amanda replied.

"Yes," she finally said. "That is probably correct."

"You know our walls cannot be rebuilt in less than a summer's time."

"Yes, Darien," Lord Ellesadil replied. "I know that."

"So," Darien replied with such energy that Will envisioned his face flushing with hope. "If your story is true, Braxidane. And the planewalkers have already cut the cord to magic, why would I not do this? Why would I not play the game of delay, which would force the Lectodinian's to expend their stores of energy before they get to the city proper? Then, once the Lectodinians' magic has been expelled— and *after* we have defeated them—turn to resolve the issue you raise?"

It was Amanda who answered.

"That plan plays with fire, Darien. There is every chance the Lectodinians would still defeat us. And if we suffer great losses in the battles you're suggesting, and if what Braxidane reports is true, we'll be unable to respond when Existence rains their fire on us."

"I've been known to gamble a bit before," Darien replied.

Braxidane broke in. "Can you play it both ways?"

"What do you mean?"

"Play your tactic. It seems wise enough. But give me your most capable mage—perhaps Amanda would join me? Let me use what magic she has to return to Existence where I belong. If I can get there, I will delay their hunt of Garrick, or perhaps even divert it. It would be a shame to lose him, after all."

"Garrick is a traitor," Darien said.

"You don't mean that," Amanda replied.

Darien drew a breath so deeply that Will could hear it through the wood. "Perhaps," he said. "And perhaps not."

"Braxidane's compromise seems wisest," Amanda said. "If I can help him, he can help us. In the meantime, we move our guard north and east. And to be truthful, what little of the Freeborn we have left can be of limited help now, anyway. Perhaps I can be of best use with him."

"You are a mage wise beyond your years, Amanda," Braxidane said. "I find myself wishing I had selected you over Garrick."

"I'll not have Garrick spoken of that way," Amanda said.

Will gave an involuntary nod from behind the door.

"All right," Darien said. "That will be the plan."

Silence came, then. A chair pushed back, and Amanda spoke. "I will meet you in my chambers in an hour."

"That would be wonderful," Braxidane replied. "In the meantime, is there anywhere I can clean up? I seem to be quite limited in my abilities right now."

"We can arrange that," Darien said.

Will had heard all he needed to hear. He glanced down the hallway again. After waiting for the outer corridor to clear, he moved from the alcove and made his way back down the servant's passageway.

He had to prepare.

And he had to get to Amanda's quarters before she and Braxidane started their spellwork.

If anyone was going to save Garrick, it was going to be him.

THIRTY-THREE

Braxidane's champions fell in line more quickly than Garrick expected, though part of that was due to the nature of time itself. The ticking of a clock, it turned out, was not as rigid as Alistair had once taught him to believe.

He found Yuli first, on the plane of Golden.

Garrick had no convincing to do with him, as the mage had already lived through enough of a life that was predicated on Braxidane's dictation. "I have no life to leave," the huge man said to Garrick upon his offer. "The sooner the better."

As it turned out, Yuli was a better mage than Garrick, and better with the sword, too—though he had no patience and weathered no fools, and for that reason alone would never find his way to drive the larger doings of a plane in any but the most blunt fashions.

They worked together to pull the vampiress Fei-ahn from Gostück.

"Why should I follow you?" she asked him as she floated in her bloody ship of magestuff. "Why should I care if the Lords of Existence do anything to us?"

"It is the right question," he answered.

She waited while he explained his own story, how he wanted to destroy the planewalker's ability to prey upon the weak. Her eyes narrowed when he told her how Braxidane's meddling caused death, pain, and destruction, and how every planewalker in Existence could reach into a plane at any time and play these games. People have enough problems as it is, he said. And he told her of the dark hunger that Braxidane had planted inside him, a hunger that let him hold power and control over others but that only served to remind him of his own self-doubt, his own lack of confidence. And then he told her of Hezarin, and the power he held within him.

As he talked, Fei-ahn's crimson eyes lidded, her jawline grew stern, and her lips turned contemplative.

"Yes," she finally said, letting her fingertips trail so seductively across the hollow of her neckline. "I have felt all of that, too. And I can see that no being in the Thousand Worlds can live freely if the *yahli-at-ba* can be as they are."

Garrick smiled at the word for "planewalker" in the Gostück language.

Yahli-at-ba was such a more apt title for a planewalker. It sounded so much more fluid than the coarser, more pedestrian language of Adruin.

"We are the only ones who can defeat the planewalkers," he said to her. "You see that, don't you? Braxidane selected us for our isolation and for our independence. Our isolation makes us weak and easily swayed, but our independence is our strength. While others see us as undesirable, or perhaps merely irrelevant, we—the strongest among us who are not tied to any single ideology—are the only ones who can even see the problem."

Fei-ahn's smile grew strangely relaxed as he spoke.

"Yes," she said when he was finished. "I see that. And I see there can be no true freedom as long as the planewalkers exercise their control. We should all be lords of our own existence."

The three of them worked together to break an uprising in Tesharia before Lelio would come with them. She reminded Garrick of Sunathri in so many ways. He liked that Lelio was a woman with other, longer names, as fitting her place as a princess of her realm, but he liked even more that she gave no quarter to those who called her anything beyond Lelio.

Yes, she was so very much like Sunathri.

He was different from each of them, though. Hezarin's essence let him play in the flow as a planewalker would, but the champions needed to learn the other way.

As every new member aligned with him, Garrick taught them each survival in the realm of Existence, how to build shells of magestuff that encased their being as they slipped through the flow, how to move, and how to sip from the waves around them to fuel their magic even further.

Once it became easy for one to slip through the flow in their cocoons of mage stuff, they split off, each gathering more champions to their side.

It was a rare champion who did not agree to join forces.

Perhaps Braxidane selected his champions for their isolation, but that same isolation served to build resentment and create a yearning for control that was strong in each of them.

Soon this band of champions from the Thousand Worlds had become a strange collection of misfits, truants, and otherwise free thinkers—all, Garrick decided, likely targeted by Braxidane when they were weak, all having needed something so badly that they would be easy marks for a planewalker's asinine doctrine of *actions and consequences.*

They were also, however, a jaded collection, each weary of the burden Braxidane had put upon them, and each more than willing to bring it to an end.

The champions split again and again, each group bringing more of their own siblings into the fold. It was only a matter of time before the Council of Joint Authority found them.

EXISTENCE

Agar came to sit in Joint Authority.

Leaxis, leader of the council flung questions at him that hung in the flow like strings of pearls.

"They are here, correct? Garrick and the rest of Braxidane's champions? You sense them, do you not?"

"Why do you ask such questions if you already know the answer?" Agar replied.

"You promised Braxidane would settle this."

"I recall making no such promise."

"You said—"

"I *said* Braxidane was trying to bring Garrick to the justice he fantasizes over. I did *not* say he would be successful."

"Semantics."

"You will fix this now."

"Me? How is this my mess?"

Leaxis flashed cold rails at him. "Do not pretend you had no plans to fill Braxidane's shoes, Agar. Consider yourself lucky that our investigation found the triggers you had set before you attempted any ill-advised efforts to take advantage of them."

Agar said nothing.

"Are you trying to start a war across All of Existence, Agar? Is that your desire?

"No, Lord Council," Agar replied. "I do not wish war."

That was true enough.

Indeed, if he had succeeded in gathering the strength he had anticipated, Agar would almost certainly have forestalled the war that was now nearly guaranteed to come. Politics across All of Exisence were tangled and twisted, and nearly assured to cause conflict. But his plan had turned to a false hope. Garrick, Braxidane's rogue champion, had broken Agar's entire structure by rallying the others.

The champions would die, of course.

Garrick and his cohort of strange magicians had no chance while fighting in the middle of Existence. But a collection of dead champions meant his original plans would have no fodder to build from, so whatever war was written into the future of the flow was going to come now, regardless of what he did.

"You will destroy Garrick," Leaxis said. "And you will destroy him now."

"It will take more than Garrick's death to staunch these wounds," Agar replied. "Spread your senses. The gates are discovered. You know better than I do that there will be more visitors."

The entire council flashed. His words were true. If the creatures of the worlds found they could survive traveling through All of Existence, the gates would see a steady flow of these same creatures invading their homeland. And that was a losing game because, while creatures of the planes bred like insects, there would be no more of the *talla*. To lose even one was bad. To open the gates to a stream of visitors would be to expose themselves to endless attacks, and that meant the only variable to extinction was time—a long time, certainly, but time is time. It moved at whatever pace one lived, and planewalkers—the *talla,* the *flow masters,* the *yahli-at-ba*—lived forever.

Now Joint Authority understood.

"So there is only one option," Leaxis finally said. "Each of Braxidane's champions must be exterminated, and their planes forever sealed."

Agar smirked. "You command an action that is certain to annoy half of Existence, and you have the nerve to suggest that *I* am the one who wants war?"

"There is no other option," Leaxis said. "The lords will see that. We will create new planes."

"I think that command goes too far," Agar replied. "Kill the champions, yes. That is a necessity. But I think the only plane that needs to die is Adruin. As it shrivels, it can fill a symbolic place in the hearts of others."

Leaxis's energy dulled as she considered the thought.

"I can agree to that," she said. "Remove the creatures who know of Existence, and make an example of Adruin. In the process, remove the cancer that is Braxidane."

Agar bowed to her in the truest purple.

"You will come with us, though, Agar, you will help us remove the stain that Braxidane has set upon us."

"Of course I will, Lord Council," Agar replied.

They left without hesitation, setting course for the node that Garrick had created, and setting course toward the champions of the Thousand Worlds.

EXISTENCE

It was when Garrick emerged from the world of Nordesta, accompanied by little Ginka, the silver-skinned being with a dark hunger that easily rivaled Garrick's own, that he felt the brunt of the Lords' attentions. It burned against him like a brand.

They knew he was here.

Garrick created his own node, then.

He waited there for his champions to emerge from their assigned worlds and he collected them up as they arrived, feeling their powers burn in the flow, feeling strength as their energy built around him.

He understood them.

He understood that they followed him not due to any edict he had made.

They followed him because he was them.

They followed him because he understood them as deeply as they loved their home worlds. They were men and women and creatures as strange as any he could recall. But he knew they stood for him because he stood for them.

"Rest," he told them as they came into his pod and shed their shells of magestuff this one last time. "Set gates and gather life force. The planewalker council will be here soon, and we must be ready."

THIRTY-FOUR

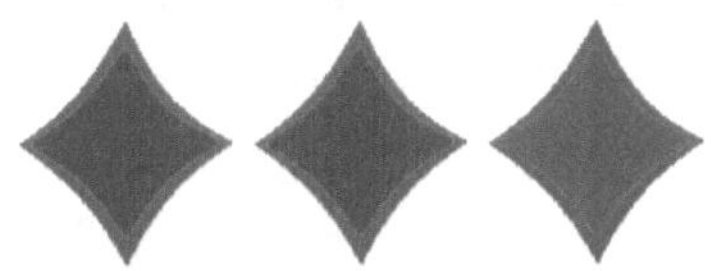

From the dirt road across the street, Will watched Braxidane approach Amanda's chambers. Upon Braxidane's entrance, however, Will crossed the road and made his way into an alleyway. From there he shimmied up a drain pipe and edged closer to Amanda's window to get an angle from which he could better hear their discussion. It was harder to hold on to the pipe these days, and he found it more difficult to steady himself against the brick wall. He was out of practice, that was for sure, but he was also getting too big for this kind of skullduggery.

Still, he was able to wedge himself into a corner and peer into the room.

He took smug satisfaction in noting that, like a hired flunky coming to his patron with his hat in his hand, the planewalker had arrived at precisely the appointed time. He couldn't help but delight in the expression that colored Braxidane's face. Even the way Braxidane carried himself when he walked showed his disgust at following such customs as keeping appointments. Yet that is exactly what he did.

When the mighty fall, Will thought, they fall hard.

Amanda's "chambers" were made of a room built above the Brass Bottom, an inn in the middle of the city. Having already met with the Freeborn and provided them their orders to support Darien, she was steeping tea and reading a manuscript as Braxidane knocked. Now the manuscript sat on a table between them, and Braxidane filled a chair across from her with his back mostly to Will's view.

"What do I need to do to help you?" she asked.

Amanda looked older than she was. The shadows of late afternoon brought lines out that weren't otherwise there. Or, perhaps it was not the lack of light that aged her, but instead the burden of leadership she had been carrying since the night Garrick defeated the planewalker and fled the city. The Freeborn were a frustrating lot during the best of times, and these were nowhere near the best of times. Will doubted Amanda had gotten more than two hours of uninterrupted sleep in days.

"Join with me," Braxidane said. "Use your reservoir and cast a link into my essence. Then let me ride along with you. Once we are traveling together I will use the life force of the plane itself to fuel your spell, and I will find a seam that will get us back into Existence."

"Find a seam?"

"Trust me," Braxidane said as he took her hands in his. "I will not lead you astray."

The words *trust me* made Will's gut do flips.

"All right," Amanda said.

The practice Will had accomplished had taught him how to be sensitive to casting, and as Amanda began to develop her spell, Will aligned himself alongside her work. He felt Braxidane pull himself into its flow, and once that was done Amanda's gasp told Will all he needed to know. Braxidane had total control of her Freeborn magic, now, and that feeling of loss was not something Amanda had expected.

Will reached into his own sense of magic and set his own self-taught gates.

He did not know how to grab energy from the area around him, but he saw how Amanda's casting disturbed the fabric of the plane. As Braxidane twisted Amanda's magic to carry the pair away, Will, too, stepped forward, moving silently into the spellwork. The pull of the casting was like a line attached to his stomach. The brick around him faded, and he felt himself … flying … flying through something that was not air.

Then the flow was a rushing current of power so hot it became hard to breathe.

Flames of color burned around him.

He wanted to scream but was afraid to reveal himself. His fingers flared, the skin on the back of his neck felt scorched. He held on, though. He couldn't stop now, so he clung to the thread Braxidane was riding on in the mere hope that he would survive.

A moment later, everything slowed and the pain faded.

His eyesight was different here—everything glowed in shifting patterns that moved with a sluggish current. He became caught up in that flow. What was it? Had it always been here?

Then he saw the gap.

It was a hole in the fabric made obvious by purple and blue smears. The smears shifted, too, they moved like they were drifting in the currents of a river. It was a leak, Will saw. The power of the plane was leaking out of that opening.

Will felt Braxidane's relief at the sight.

"Ah, Garrick, my young upstart," Braxidane said. "I thank myself that you are as predictable as you are resourceful."

Will stirred as he felt the essence of Master Garrick in the flow.

His motion brought attention.

"Will?" Braxidane said.

"That's right."

"What are you doing here?" Amanda said.

"I …" Will wasn't sure what to say. "I'm going to be with Garrick."

Braxidane laughed.

"Take him back," Amanda demanded.

"Actions and consequences," Braxidane said. "There is no time now for that now. The boy has cast his die."

Will felt Amanda's attempt to wrest control of her magic back from the planewalker, but Braxidane was in his element now and would not be heeded. She cried out, but the three of them still traveled toward the seam.

"Stop fighting me," Braxidane said to her. "Your struggles serve only to make matters worse for you."

And, though Amanda did not stop struggling, Braxidane gathered them both into his power and stepped them through that tiny snip in the fabric that led to All of Existence.

EXISTENCE

Leaxis flowed on a trail that burned with the sickly sweet smell of sugar on fire. The rest of the planewalker council, Lar, Valpu-nof, Wadanti, and others arrived just behind.

Garrick saw no need to speak.

Both he and Leaxis understood that the planewalkers could not afford to leave any champion standing and that the champions had come to Existence specifically to rid the Thousand Worlds of their planewalker oversight.

Both understood this would be a battle to the death.

Garrick flared a red and blue symbol.

They turned to him then, the champions—a force greater than any before seen in any one of the Thousand Worlds alone.

"To your gates," Garrick said, reaching into the flow and ripping energy together to form a sword of flaming power. "It is time to rid ourselves of these parasites."

The champions jettisoned themselves from the node and spread across Existence, each taking positions between the planewalkers and the gate that led to their home worlds.

Leaxis wrapped herself around Garrick, hoping to snuff him with one quick burst, but he was no longer a simple mage. He used Hezarin's spite against her kinsfolk, and cut into the Lord Council with the sword.

Leaxis retreated, licking her wounds.

Garrick flowed forward, part man, part planewalker, striding through the vast pit of magestuff and life force and the other fledgling flanges of power he had never before felt. It was as if All of Existence wrapped around him. As if he could reach out and touch any part of it.

The battle engaged everywhere at once.

Champions screamed. Planewalkers threw energy through multi-space with prismatic flashes in spectrums that Garrick had never before seen.

As he waded on, he felt a new ripple in the flow, a green bubble of darkness that raced across a hemisphere of his thought. Braxidane. It was Braxidane. And it was Amanda, and ... he sensed a third essence, a thin yellow presence that tasted of mint and beat with a power that grew stronger as each segment of time passed.

Will?

His sword flared.

What was Will doing here?

Leaxis sent a crackling wall of thunder and lightning screeching through the distance between them.

Garrick shielded himself, then cut into Leaxis.

All of Existence shook with rage.

She responded by tossing greater flows of power at him. The fabric of time tore with the sound of banshees on fire. The council came forward to fight beside her, while other *talla* suddenly appeared nearby, peeling off toward gates of the Thousand Worlds in numbers too great to count.

Three of the planewalkers underestimated the champions and died immediately, and two others fled. But more stood and fought their bloody battles, bringing cries from the champions.

Garrick caught Valpu-nof distracted, and All of Existence shuddered as the planewalker's essence imploded into many-space. Garrick reached into the core of the explosion and mixed Valpunof's energy with Hezarin's. He absorbed Lar next but left Leaxis an opening. Only a nimble reaction saved him from the lord council's attack.

More planewalkers appeared, some skimming off to battle the champions, others staying to join the struggle against Garrick.

And some, Garrick saw, had turned on others.

The planewalkers were fighting each other, turning the melee from a pure rebellion to some odd mixture of prison break and civil war. It made him laugh as he fought. It buoyed his spirit to see these "gods" in their most insane forms.

He blocked spell work and fended off attacks.

He waved his sword in wide swaths of destruction.

He cried and screamed as, around him, explosions ripped the very fabric of Existence.

Understanding dawned slowly.

He was stronger than any one of them.

His humanity had built upon the *talla* essence he had taken from Hezarin to create something different, something unique—and that uniqueness was something the planewalkers had never had to deal with before.

They adjusted and learned, though. And in tactics that reminded him of Adruin's mages of the orders, some began to gather together and fight as one.

Still, the battle raged.

Braxidane shed the weight of the boy and the Torean mage as he flowed through Garrick's node.

He watched as the melee became a tangled mess of chaos between groups that shifted with every moment. It was a maelstrom of power, a conglomeration of magic, weaponry, blood, and death, unlike anything he could have imagined.

This was not what he had wanted.

It wasn't right. And worse, it was going to ruin his entire plan. What value was leading All of Existence if All of Existence was nothing but a hollow shadow of its former self? Why were his brothers and sisters ruining everything? What had the champions done?

"Stop it!" Braxidane screamed as he stepped into the void.

But the flash of his voice and the taste of his tone were lost in the churn. Braxidane pulsed green and orange and yellow, and he reeked of pure honey. He took on the form of a flaming eagle, talons outstretched to lean into an onrushing wave of energy as he landed.

"Stop this!" he called again. "Brothers! Sisters! You're ruining everything!"

"Now you choose to see the truth, brother?" Agar said from his place at Adruin's gate.

"These are my champions!" Braxidane called. "If you leave them be, I will bring this to an end!"

Agar laughed. "You don't see the truth even now?"

"I can control them."

"No, Braxidane. "That time is long past."

Agar ripped the seal away from Adruin, then, and he tossed it aside in a bloody haze of mist and gore. He laughed at Braxidane again. "You are done brother," he said. "It is time for your consequence."

Agar launched himself like a missile into the middle of Braxidane's being.

The blast pulsed with power. A moment later, particles of Braxidane's life force scattered across the expanse of Existence.

It was as if everything inside Garrick had been ripped from its place —his heart tore, his liver shredded, his lungs... He wanted to scream, but the pain was so intense there was nothing left to scream with. He froze in pain, his back arched, his fists clenched around the pommel of his flaming sword.

Leaxis whipped him then, too.

She spun in a whirling cloud that sent streams from her hair to sear his ribs and raise welts that burned like salted wounds.

It was a pain like none other, but when it ended Garrick felt a freedom he had never known could exist.

Braxidane was gone.

He was free. Truly free.

He was free of Braxidane. Free of Alistair, and fee of Hersha Padiglio. Free of Elman and the orders. Free of Darien and Ellesadil. Free of Sunathri. Free of his mother, of Baron Fahid, and of every other man who had ever owned him. He was past them, now.

This was his life. The idea tasted true and pure.

Leaxis cried out then.

She had Amanda crushed in a power vise. The Freeborn mage fought valiantly, but she was losing. The truth of her fate registered as raw fear in the deepness of her eyes.

But Will came behind Leaxis and cut into her grasp.

Her hold on Amanda broke, but the planewalker stunned the boy so that he hung there, suspended in mid-space, spinning away in silence, arms and legs trailing away into nothingness.

Garrick cried out and raced toward them, lobbing great handfuls of energy at her. Three lords died in his attack, but Leaxis shied away and survived.

She let go of Will, though.

Garrick poured himself into the boy and was encouraged when his life force surged. It felt like summer, he thought. The boy was pure of heart. His essence felt like summer.

He would have grown into a good man if Garrick had not conspired with the planewalkers to destroy his future.

There was no time to dwell, though. The lords pressed in on him, their combined presence like a net closing over him. He pressed against that curtain and felt the lack of trust at its seams.

That was it.

The planewalkers held no love for each other. They could not trust. At their core, they lived lives of fear. They wanted only control, only power. And since ultimate power corrupts, they would never be able to give trust.

But they were like insects, too.

Or, to use Braxidane's more apt analogy, the planewalkers were weeds, simple shells for power, conduits that could lie fallow for centuries, for millennia, for eons, and still would come back as soon as the energy of Existence were to filter through them. He felt this in the planewalker life force that he held inside his body. The foundation of a planewalker was undying, and as Braxidane had once suggested of a plane, they would always come back.

Unless.

Garrick gave a grim expression as he cast magic.

Unless they were truly obliterated.

Unless every trace of them was removed from the world as one, single, whole.

"Amanda!" Garrick called as he threw more energy at the council "Recover Will! Protect him!"

Amanda moved toward where the boy lay in stasis, floating in a maelstrom cloud of the essence that was All of Existence, and Garrick turned back to the battle.

He saw devastation.

And he saw, also, the truth of the struggle. The supply of planewalkers seemed endless, but his champions were not. They were dying and would not last much longer no matter how one counted time.

His champions were going to be destroyed.

He pushed himself throughout the entirety that was All of Existence then. The movement was instinctive and simple. He spread himself into a vaporous energy that filled the full extent of every-where at once.

"Run," he flashed at the champions. "Take to your planes!"

And they did.

He covered their retreats, spreading himself farther as he grasped for anything he could touch and dragged himself further into every open space throughout All of Existence. He reached into dimensions to set gates. He pulled energy from Talin and drank directly from Existence itself, mixing it all with power that came from his own life force. He was the air. He was the smoke that filled every space in that air. Time bent. Infinite existence came as a vision that was crystalline and clear. Land collapsed below him. He felt Amanda and Will. He felt planewalkers and nodes. The champions were retreating, and the essence of the dead swirled in the reaches of this many-space. A siren called from a place he could not determine. A low rumble filled the void.

Did he exist anymore?

Did he have a body?

Yes. No. He had no words for this existence. No framework for this consciousness. All he knew was that he was there. Ubiquitous. Ready.

Leaxis cast a flame into the framework of his node then.

Garrick latched onto it.

He clenched every part of himself, grabbed every planewalker he came into contact with, and pulled them all tight against him. He condensed, and a vacuum throughout All of Existence ripped into the very essence of each of them. He swallowed it all into himself. Power crammed into his gates, crushing them, stretching them, rending them.

He wrapped himself tightly around the Lord Council.

The planewalker's fire flared brightly.

She screamed, but her voice was drowned by a rasping torrent of power that collapsed into itself faster than Garrick could control.

Space drew down, condensing, compressing into heat and energy.

There was an explosion.

A thousand bitter-sharp knives bore into him.

His brain collapsed. Gates tore and crumbled like the wall around Dorfort. Was this his mind cracking? Was it his body? Pain centered on a single point. Exquisite pain. Intense pain. Pain that drew into a scream that echoed throughout all of Existence.

Then it was done, and there was nothing but a dark and solid silence.

THIRTY-FIVE

Zutrian Esta was reviewing supply plans with his counselors when his link to the plane of magic returned. It came with such a jolt that he nearly dropped the parchment he had been reading.

The others felt it, too.

The link. Fresh and pure. It filled his senses with joyous excitement.

He set a gate and cast a faint breeze over the page before him, smiling as the force cooled his skin and the page turned to a new table of figures.

He looked into the beaming faces of his compatriots.

"Does this mean what I think it does?" said Haffee.

"Yes." It was Cara who replied. "The link has returned, just as I expected it would."

Zutrian nodded.

The scars that crossed Cara's face and neck spoke for her understanding of how things could work throughout the planes. Cara had been the strongest voice on his panel and had argued long that the power would return. She said she understood the creatures who controlled magic, and that it would not be in their best interests to withhold it forever.

Zutrian demurred to her in this case because he agreed with her. He had dealt with powerful entities across planes before. They understood that business did not work well when lines of commerce were cut.

But inside, Zutrian admitted he was relieved. He had not been as sure of himself as he let on. This event meant he could relax. It meant their advantage was real.

He turned to Cara.

"You were right to take such a position, Cara. I think it is time you step further into a role that guides this order. If you would, please go and gather the council together for a session this evening. It is time to launch our attack on Dorfort, and I would like you to lead it."

She did a poor job of fighting a grin.

"I would be honored to take such a role, High Superior."

"Then go gather the order. We must ride soon."

EXISTENCE

"Gather them up," a champion said to Amanda.

"What?" Amanda finally managed to reply. She had been in a fog of thought.

The champion was female, dressed in black armor that was scorched and otherwise worse for wear after the battle, and carrying a mace that glowed with a muted flare.

"We are returning to our planes," another champion replied—a male this time, a man with pale orange skin and who was slight of bearing. He had multiple eye sockets ringing the half circle around the ridge of his forehead. "You need to take Garrick and your other partner to your plane."

Amanda nodded, comprehension finally coming together.

The battle was done. The champions had returned to the space that was All of Existence now. The planewalkers were gone, defeated somehow. In their place was a small pebble, or a marble, spinning madly in a tight circle, spitting and sizzling in flashes and flares of energy. It felt massively dense, though, somehow huge despite its size. Looking at it gave Amanda a strange sense of vertigo.

The champion who spoke was named Fei-ahn and had fought closely by Garrick.

Amanda saw Garrick then, prone and floating in the void, his arms and legs extended in graceful repose. He did not seem to breathe, but she felt stirring inside him.

What had he done?

Was he alive?

And she saw Will, also floating in the multi-space, also still shocked and dazed but rousing and trying to pull himself together. The boy muttered incoherent phrases that she had no way to understand. Neither Garrick nor Will had a protective shell of mage stuff—which did not surprise her in Garrick's case but made her pause for the boy, though in her state of confusion she could not say why that would bother her.

She put her hand to her head and steadied herself.

"Does Garrick still live?" she asked.

"I do not know," the woman replied. "But he deserves to return to the plane of his home."

"I don't know what he considers home," Amanda replied.

The faces of the champions took on expressions that varied from frowns to scowls to knowing grins. "We understand," Fei-ahn said. "Are you able to take him to Adruin, though?" the woman asked. "We think he would want to be there."

"Yes," she replied. "I can do that."

Her body shook as she collected both Will and Garrick to her. It felt as if she might break something each time she moved, but she brought both of them into her shell and traversed through the flow of Existence until she came to Adruin's gate.

"If he lives, tell Garrick we will tell his tale on Gostück," the dark-clad woman said. "And that I'm sure others will do the same."

"I will," she mumbled as she peered back into the dark beauty of Existence.

It was the first time, and possibly the last, that she would be able to fully look at it. She took it in like a surveyor would. Exploring its vast ocean of emptiness, of darkness made of pure scents and tastes and other senses she could not describe. Energy still welled her. Power still snapped in the emptiness of the many-space that lay below it. That power curled in on itself, billowing in waves and stray rays of light. It was like the night sky, she thought, only deeper.

She felt hope, then.

She felt opportunity.

Existence was strong, she thought.

Existence was bold, warm, and chilling. Other words came to her, too. Powerful. Breathtaking. Delicate.

Dangerous.

Before coming here, Amanda had thought she was strong. She thought she knew what she was doing, and why she was doing it. She thought she had understood what life was about. She had been through battle, after all. She had seen leaders like Darien and Reynard. Like Garrick. And she had seen the ways that power would corrupt a person. She considered herself good, a wise person for her years.

Yet, as she took in the depths of Existence she felt an overwhelming sense of awe that very nearly brought her to her knees.

This was why life is so bitterly beautiful.

"I will tell him of your tales," she said to Fei-ahn and the rest of the champions. "And I will tell him of your victories."

Then Amanda did as the remaining champions did, she pulled Garrick and Will with her as she slipped into the gate that led back to her world.

THIRTY-SIX

Darien cursed. He was tired and his head hurt. Mostly, though, he wanted to reach out and throttle someone. There was, however, no one here to throttle. He looked at the map where he had outlined the coming battle.

He had three mages.

That was it.

Once it became understood that Amanda, too, had left Dorfort, the rest of the Freeborn had scattered to the winds. He had retained the three only by promising them a thief's ransom.

Not that it would matter.

The Lectodinians would bring thousands of men and cartloads of mages. He could slow them without sustaining great losses as they came from the East Mists, but the terrain from there to the rivers was too flat to support the ambushes he would need, and with only three mages to fall back on he couldn't plan any surprises there.

That left only the surrounding woodlands in which to set traps, all of which had now been built. They were a poor shield for a city that still had no wall, however.

He clenched his fist and pressed it against his temple as he went to the window to breathe fresh air.

This was Garrick's fault.

The end was near.

It would not be long before Zutrian Esta's forces would arrive.

He thought of his father and his brother, both of whom had spent their lives in the service of this city. He leaned against the window sill and looked down, trying hard but failing to keep from seeing himself as the failure he was.

A commotion brewed in the manor yard.

People gathered, their voices rising in general unrest that set him on edge. One man dragged his son away and pointed toward the government center. The boy sprinted him across the yard, holding his hat to his head as he went to the guard outside.

The only word Darien heard was his name being called.

The boy had asked for him.

He sighed and straightened, doing his best to ignore the wave of fatigue that washed over him. There was always some new problem.

His hand went to his father's sword, which he now kept at his side at all times.

Boot steps came from the corridor, then a knock came at the door. He glanced a last time at the crowd of people and saw a face he recognized.

Amanda.

"Commander J'ravi?" the voice echoed.

"Enter," he said, turning.

The boy was there, chest heaving from his run, hat in hand. The guard stood beside him. "Sorry to interrupt, Commander," the guard said.

"It's Garrick, sir," the boy said. "He has returned."

Darien's heart jumped, but something in the boy's face darkened his excitement.

"What is wrong?"

"He's injured, sir. My pa says ..."

But Darien had already stepped past the boy and into the hallway.

"Bring an apothecary," he told the guard as he raced from the chamber.

His boot heels sank into the grassy soil as he ran across the manor. Amanda was kneeling over Garrick's prone form. The god-touched mage was pale and gaunt, his hair matted into oily chunks, his skin drawn tight over his sharp cheekbones, his lips bloodless.

Will, too, was there, lying on his side and murmuring.

"Darien," Amanda said, rising.

"Bring a pallet," Darien barked at a member of the guard who had come near. "What happened?" he asked Amanda.

"I ..." she gazed around the gathering. "Perhaps we could discuss this once we get Garrick and the boy settled."

Darien nodded.

A detail of the guard appeared, the apothecary running behind with a cart of the phials and ceramic bowls of his administrations clattering in the afternoon air.

"I'm sorry to see you again so soon, Commander," the apothecary said, obviously referring to Darien's father.

"Me, too," Darien replied. "Get him to a comfortable place."

A SHORT WHILE LATER, with Garrick comfortably resting but still unresponsive, Amanda and Darien retired to his war room. He offered food and drink, which Amanda partook of. Will came with her, still sullen and dazed but recovering and unwilling to be left out of the conversation. He did not eat. He did not speak. He did not react as the captains and other staff milled about the room attending to their duties.

Darien looked at Will as he took a seat beside the map table.

"Are you sure he's all right?"

Amanda nodded grimly. "I hope so. But I want him near me now, and, regardless, he deserves to hear this."

Darien raised his eyebrows but said nothing more on the subject.

"You can see my problem," he indicated the map, which showed the overwhelming numbers the Lectodinians would bring.

"I don't need to see the map to understand your problem," Amanda said. "I know the mages are coming."

"True enough, but this map is useful because it helps one see that my biggest issue is getting the Torean Freeborn to hold up their end of our bargain."

"How many remain?"

Darien snuffed and pulled at his tunic.

"We have three mages. Four, counting you."

"Then you have three mages."

Darien looked at Amanda. Something was different about her now. There was a new depth to her gaze that he had not seen before.

"You see this, don't you," she said. "How ridiculous this is? Somewhere in your heart? Tell me you see that it doesn't matter how many mages you have. And it doesn't matter how many mages the Lectodinians have. All you're going to do either way is to kill a lot of people and destroy a collection of families."

"Tell that to the Lectodinians."

"Someone should."

"Good luck with that."

Amanda smiled in a failed attempt to cut tension. Yes, Darien thought as he took her in more fully.

"What has happened to you?" Darien asked.

She set her lips and looked as if she was trying to find words. Her expression made him angry. It said he was deficient. It said he couldn't possibly understand what she was thinking.

"We are our own worst enemy, Darien," she said, her voice trailing away. "Just as the planewalkers were their own worst enemy. Do you see that?"

"I see that mages from the north will destroy Dorfort in less than a week if the Toreans won't help. I see death and devastation."

"Death and devastation are coming either way. The world is too vast for drawing these kinds of lines. They are just mages, Darien. They must need something. How can we justify losing half our people defending a piece of dirt when we don't even know what the Lectodinians actually want? How many of the Lectodinian mages who are in the attack force, for example, actually think they are doing right by rolling over the land, and how many are here only because their leaders are driving them? How many are blindly following when they would prefer instead to find other ways?"

She stared at him with her blue eyes steeled now.

"How many would be willing to die for the Lectodinian order if they knew who we were, or what a shared future might look like? It's not like Zutrian Esta himself is storming our broken gate now, is it? What would it take for Zutrian to put his own life on the line?"

"I understand," Darien growled.

"What do you understand?"

"I understand you are enjoying a little thought game, and I understand you would see us all murdered before you would lift a finger to help."

"Then you don't see well at all."

Amanda came to stand before him.

"You are a good man, Darien. But you are misguided. You draw your boundaries in whatever way makes you most comfortable. You see nothing beyond what you will see, and you are too stubborn to change."

Darien gritted his teeth. "Perhaps that's true Amanda, but our city lives on because of men like me. Backing away from such a threat as the Lectodinians, as you would have me do, puts every life in Dorfort at risk."

"I'm not suggesting we back away," she snapped.

Darien chuffed a cynical laugh. Amanda's expression turned to one of pity, which served only to infuriate Darien further. He drew a breath and was about to tear into her when Will stood up and went to the map.

THIRTY-SEVEN

Darien and Amanda's voices echoed in the distance but Will paid them no mind.

He thought, instead, of Garrick lying now in his bed chamber with physicians and nursemaids hovering over him. Garrick would live, he thought, though Will knew he would probably never be the same. And he felt the thing that Garrick had left inside him. Yes, he felt it. It was a connection to Existence, a link that filled his chest in a way that he could not miss.

Garrick had triggered him.

It had to have been Garrick. His master's presence seemed woven into that link. It smelled of him. It had his strength. His personality. But mostly Will knew it had to be Garrick's doing because Garrick had once promised he would teach Will magic, and because Garrick had never before let him down.

It must have been while they were in All of Existence. After he had been hurt. Probably when Garrick saved him. Whenever its source, though, Will could say only that it had come, and that he knew it was here.

He set a gate and let a sugary rush score his being.

It sent a shiver through him that made him gasp. It felt different than the smaller magics he had cast before. Finally, he heard Amanda's voice cut into his thoughts.

What would it take for Zutrian to put his own life on the line?

He opened his eyes, then. Full and wide. The argument continued around him, but Will stared at the map.

He wanted to see.

He wanted to understand.

He stood up, then, and as the voices of Darien and Amanda fell silent, went to the table.

It was a model of Adruin raised in relief, complete with the lake painted in waves. The city of Dorfort was nestled in the arms of the three rivers that wound their way from the northern territories of the Vapor Peaks and of the mountains that encircled the Desert of Dust, where Arderveer had been, and where Will knew Commander J'ravi and Master Garrick had first clashed with mages of the orders.

Darien's captains had set blue markers on the map to mark out the Lectodinian forces, positioning them, Will was certain, based on reports from advanced scouts and from other citizens. Dorfort's forces were colored a burnt orange.

The Lectodinian's were too vast.

Images of bloodshed flashed through his mind. He saw Elman with a knife in his chest, a knife that Will himself had thrown. He saw Ettril Dor-Entfar lying in a pool of his own blood. He recalled the night of terror brought by Hezarin and her liege Neuma, and he remembered Hezarin so publicly sacrificing Neuma when it became convenient to do so.

The map foretold of more bloodshed.

More sacrifice.

His gaze went to the model of the northern mountains.

Zutrian Esta, High Superior of the Lectodinian order, was probably sitting in the center of those mountains right now. He was probably looking at a map no different from this one. Will's chest tingled. It was strange to breathe. He felt close to Zutrian Esta, somehow. His mind seemed to spread toward the north, then, and he felt a power rise in him that he did not understand.

"Amanda was right," he said almost to himself.

That was when he noticed Amanda and Darien staring at him.

He smiled. Then he cleared his throat and took a firmer stance.

He knew what he needed to do.

Will set a gate, and funneled the essence of All of Existence through it. He felt the familiar flavor of magic fill him. But this was a free power, oddly unencumbered. It was a power that flowed straight from Existence rather than funneled through the plane of magic.

It warmed him as it pooled in his chest.

He channeled it and opened another gate.

It felt strange to work with such freeform impulse, but he knew what he was doing as he followed the flow—or at least he knew what he was going to do. He understood it as surely as if Garrick himself was in the seat directly behind him, piloting his raft. He was comfortable with this power, familiar with it in an odd way.

He focused on a mountain to the north, a place inhabited by the only person on the plane who could change this.

Then Will put his hand into the air, spoke a word of magic, and stepped into time itself.

THIRTY-EIGHT

Will emerged in the middle of a cavern.

It was a comfortable place, well-lit by afternoon sunlight that filtered through the open gap that looked out over the rugged mountainscape. Benches lay scattered about, and the residue of magic combined with the bright light to give the space a sharpness. It smelled of warm oil. Tables and other counters held the trappings of spellwork.

Zutrian Esta was dressed in a simple outfit of dark pants and a shirt of blue fabric.

"I told you," he said, wheeling angrily toward Will, "I wanted to be alone!"

He started at Will's presence, then stammered. "What …?"

"Zutrian Esta?" Will said.

The high superior stood taller and glanced at the closed door behind Will.

"Who are you?"

Will smiled. "It doesn't really matter, now, does it?"

The Lectodinian prepared a spell.

Will let his mind follow Zutrian's work, and timed his casting to divert the flow of magestuff away before it could bloom. It was easy. This link Garrick had left inside him was faster than the ties to Talin, and it was fueled by the grander energies of the Thousand Worlds. It was almost the same as casting while in Existence itself.

Zutrian's face grew ashen.

"What do you want?"

"I want you to call back your attack on Dorfort. And any other you might have planned across the rest of the plane."

Zutrian laughed.

"You just felt what I'm capable of."

Zutrian grew smug. "I don't care who you are, boy. You can't stop Dorfort from falling."

"You're right about that. I'm just one mage. And a new one at that. Even though I'm faster than you and probably stronger than you, I can't defeat the whole of your forces alone. But, you see, Master Esta, I think you're making one very big mistake."

"And that would be?"

"You are assuming I would fight to save Dorfort."

"But ..."

"Oh, don't get me wrong. I like Dorfort just fine. I want it to be safe. I have friends there." He thought about Garrick. "Family, even. But you're probably right about what would happen if I *fought* to save Dorfort. I'm sure you would win—even a simple boy like me can do those maths."

Zutrian sat against the edge of the table. An indulgent smile crawled over his lips. "So ... what are you doing here?"

"Here's what you are going to do," Will said. "You are going to contact your leaders, and you are going to call off the attack. If you don't do this right now, I will kill you."

"You understand," Zutrian said, his face growing smug. "That killing me—assuming that were even possible—will not stop my Lectodinians. They will still control Dorfort, and therefore the whole plane of Adruin."

"I don't think you're listening," Will replied.

"I'm listening just fine."

"Not really. If you were listening, you would understand that if I have to kill you, I will then go to your next in charge, and I will offer that same agreement. And if I must kill that leader, I'll continue to work my way down your chain until I find someone who will decide to stop this thing. It's really that simple."

Will kept his gaze firm on Zutrian's. When, after several beats, the Lectodinian High Superior had not replied, he added. "If you chose that option, I suppose that, if nothing else, we'll discover how deep the commitment your leaders to your cause goes."

"You're just a boy," Zutrian said as a redness came to his cheeks.

Power rose within the Lectodinian, and Will shut it down once again. He didn't know how long he could draw on Existence, but he hoped it was a good sign that he wasn't feeling tired.

"Boy or not, I've killed mages of your order who were planning to murder my friends before," Will said. "I will have no problems doing it again."

Zutrian glared, then. He stood taller and smoothed his shirts. "Be gone," he said. "I have no more time to waste on you," He strode toward the doorway.

Will flowed Existence through his gates, and the door slammed shut.

Zutrian whirled. He hesitated, then took a step toward Will.

Will cast a golden barrier between them.

Zutrian, racing forward, crashed headfirst into it before collapsing into a heap on the floor.

"Halsten!" he called.

"As I was saying, Master Esta," Will said. "I do not intend to fight your forces, but I will ensure that every man or woman who is ultimately responsible for the pain and suffering that will happen as a result of his or her order—will be dead. Perhaps this is fine with you. Maybe you are willing to give your life for your vision. But you have to realize that what I am going to do means that your vision of a world ruled by Lectodinians will occur only if every member of your staff—every single one—is equally strong in their belief in that future as you are, or only if the people in your armies are so dedicated to your goals that they will fight to make it all happen without such a command."

Zutrian Esta picked himself off the floor in an awkward series of ginger movements. He was an old man, Will saw. A man who was afraid.

A rumbling came to the door, but it did not open.

Zutrian's brow knitted.

"Why are you doing this?"

"Do you think every member of your staff believes as you do? Are they all willing to make such a sacrifice? Do you think they will all die for your cause?"

Zutrian stammered.

Will smiled, enjoying the expression on the high superior's face as the picture he had drawn fell into place. At the same moment, he raised an open palm, letting the essence of Existence pool in it, watching as the power sparked in ways that caught Zutrian's full attention. Will thought about Darien and Amanda back in the war chamber. He thought about Garrick, and about the rest of the champions across the Thousand Worlds as he raised his glowing magestuff high enough to bring deep shadows to the lines that marked age on the Lectodinian's face.

"I don't know what your people will say," Will continued. "But, of course, the only question that matters right now is this one: Zutrian Esta, High Superior of the Lectodinian order of mages, are *you* willing to die for your cause, or are we going to call this thing off?"

Zutrian gave him a cold glare. Then he took a single breath and cast his eyes downward.

Will smiled.

"All right, then," he said. "Let's get this thing shut down."

EPILOGUE

Garrick opened his eyes. He was lying on his side. The sheets felt like stone against his legs. His ribs burned with pain so sharp that even shallow breathing hurt. He was warm, despite the cool breeze from the window across the room, a breeze that carried hints of the Blue Lake.

The aroma of cold soup came from the stand beside his bed.

He felt empty inside, broken in some basic way that he couldn't understand. Braxidane's magic had been ripped from him when the planewalkers had died. That did not surprise him. He assumed it would happen. But his own Torean magic—the structure of his gates, and the ability to call to the plane of magic—was also torn and tattered. He felt its loss as if it were a broken bone somewhere deep inside him.

Unlike a real bone, though, Garrick didn't think this would heal.

His magic was gone.

All of it. But the planewalkers were gone, too. Forever. He lay back and let the ramifications of that roll over him. It felt good. He had won his freedom. Whatever that meant.

Both Amanda and Darien had been in to speak with him earlier, so he knew the walls around the government center still lay in ruins, but also that the city of Dorfort still stood. He knew the Lectodinians had stood down, and that Will had something to do with it. The constant jangle of war harnesses in the lane outside all morning stood testimony to the fact that Dorfort was still on alert, but fear of imminent war seemed to have been quelled.

A nurse brought him a fresh tray, then retreated.

Once he thought he was alone, Garrick rolled over to find Will sitting in a chair propped against the far wall.

"You're awake?" Will said.

Garrick nodded. "As that is." He pulled himself up to something closer to a sitting position, his shoulders, at least, against the wall behind him.

The boy seemed taller. His angular body seemed bigger.

"I understand the Lectodinians have not come," Garrick said.

"No," Will replied. "I had a conversation with Lord Esta. I don't expect they will be attacking anyone any time soon."

Garrick smiled despite his pain. "I knew you could do it."

"It was nothing more than you would have done."

"Hmm."

Will sat forward and the chair came to a rest on the floor. "What did you do to me?"

"What do you mean?"

"Don't be like the planewalkers," Will said, his voice growing firm. "You knew I would be linked when you were finished."

"No." Garrick shook his head. "That is not true."

Knowing Will was here was beginning to make him feel better. He motioned Will to help him with the soup. Will spooned some. The simple tastes of broth and fowl made him happy.

"I didn't know if it would work," he finally said. "But I admit I hoped as much. You'll be a fine mage, Will. You are young, but you are the right person for this responsibility."

"But I have no sponsor now, thanks to you and the champions."

"Even better."

"What do you mean?"

"You are a champion like none other, Will. Your magic comes from Existence itself, but you are tied to no one. You are beholden to no higher power."

"Will you teach me what you know?"

Garrick's smile was almost wistful. "What I can. You should learn from everyone, though. That's how Sunathri would have had you learn. You'll be a stronger mage for it."

Will nodded. "You will always be my superior," he said.

"I'm not sure that's such a good thing."

"I am."

Garrick smiled, and this time spooned the soup himself. He put the bowl down, and stretched his arms, wincing at the pain. At least he could breathe a bit now. That much was good. "The people won't see it that way, though," he said. "People don't change."

Will shrugged. "Darien says that people change as the world around them does."

Garrick thought about that.

Perhaps it was true. It would make him feel better if it were true, anyway.

There would still be problems. Conflict would still come, and some men would always strive to take advantage of others. It was the way of people. But at least now there would be no planewalkers to interfere in their ways, and with Will holding the politicians at bay perhaps the people stood a chance to decide for themselves what was right. Garrick thought about Sunathri, a woman he now knew beyond doubt that he would have loved had they had the proper time together. She would be happy.

He nodded to himself and looked at the boy.

Will was Adruin's champion now.

He was a young man who had grown up in this world, and who would shape it in whatever way was to come.

"You're a good man, Will," he said.

He hoped that would last forever.

This is the end of *God Mage.* I greatly value feedback. If you have enjoyed this story so far, please consider returning to your favorite booksellers and leaving a review.

The story of Garrick, Darien, and the struggle between the orders continues in *Champion Mage,* available as another tenth-anniversary edition of *Saga of the God-Touched Mage.*

The Saga of the God-Touched Mage
(10th Anniversary Edition)
includes

Apprentice Mage
Rogue Mage
Champion Mage
God Mage

Acknowledgments

The universe of Adruin and All of Existence has many people to thank for its existence, not the least of which are Tim Brown, Mike Cox, Ken and Jackie Peters, and my wife, Lisa.

I need to single out a few others for their efforts beyond all the rest.

My friend, collaborator, and pre-reader John Bodin's help was—as always—superlative. I want to thank my daughter, Brigid, for stepping into the fray when I needed her. And I want to give thanks to both my original cover artist, Rachel Carpenter, who was great fun to work with and who did a fantastic job bringing Garrick to life, and to Lisa Silverthorne who blew my mind with her great work on this 10th Anniversary edition.

Mostly, though, I have to thank Lisa for everything she's done for me. *Saga of the God-Touched Mage* has gone through more twists and turns than I could ever have predicted when the idea first hit, and she's been with me through every step. (Don't worry, honey. It's really done. Really, I mean it. It's done. You don't have to read it for the 111th time!).

About Ron Collins

Ron Collins is a bestselling Science Fiction and Dark Fantasy author who writes across the spectrum of speculative fiction.

Both his science fiction series, *Stealing the Sun*, and his fantasy series, *Saga of the God-Touched Mage*, have been bestsellers. His short fiction has received a Writers of the Future prize. He has published numerous short stories in venues such as *Analog, Asimov's, Pulphouse*, and the *Fiction River* original anthology project. His short stories have been listed on the preliminary ballot for SFWA's Nebula Award, and "The White Game" was nominated for the Short Mystery Fiction Society's Derringer Award.

His latest books are *Home Run Enchanted, Curveball Cursed*, and *Outfield Magicked*, which comprise the Fairies and Fastballs series, written with his daughter.

NEWSLETTER & CONTACT

Discover other work by Ron Collins at:
https://www.typosphere.com

Join Ron's Reader List, and get free books!:
https://typosphere.com/newsletter